Cal Jamieson had been dour, if not downright hostile, ever since he'd arrived

Not that the children seemed to find him nearly as intimidating as she did. They were still squealing with laughter as he showed them his favorite trick.

Then, unable to keep a straight face at the twins' delight any longer, Cal smiled.

Who would have guessed that cool mouth could crease his face with such charm, that the steely look could dissolve into warmth and humor?

Juliet didn't want him to be attractive. Somehow it was easier to think that he was always cold and hostile than to know that he was nice to children. But she couldn't help wondering. Would he ever smile at *her* the way he smiled at them?

Jessica Hart had a haphazard career before she began writing to finance a degree in history. Her experiences ranged from waitress, theater production assistant and outback cook to newsdesk secretary, expedition assistant and English teacher, and she has worked in countries as different as France and Indonesia, Australia and Cameroon. She now lives in the north of England, where her hobbies are limited to eating and drinking and traveling when she can, preferably to places where she'll find good food or desert or tropical rain.

Don't miss any of our special offers. Write to us at the following address for information on our newest releases.

Harlequin Reader Service
U.S.: 3010 Walden Ave., P.O. Box 1325, Buffalo, NY 14269
Canadian: P.O. Box 609, Fort Erie, Ont. L2A 5X3

Outback Husband
Jessica Hart

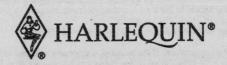

HARLEQUIN®

TORONTO • NEW YORK • LONDON
AMSTERDAM • PARIS • SYDNEY • HAMBURG
STOCKHOLM • ATHENS • TOKYO • MILAN • MADRID
PRAGUE • WARSAW • BUDAPEST • AUCKLAND

ISBN 0-373-03594-2

OUTBACK HUSBAND

First North American Publication 2000.

This edition published by arrangement with Harlequin Books S.A.

Visit us at www.romance.net

Printed in U.S.A.

CHAPTER ONE

'MUMMY, someone's coming!'

Wiping her hands on her apron, Juliet came out of the kitchen and shaded her eyes against the glare as she watched the tell-tale column of red dust that signalled a vehicle speeding towards them along the dusty track.

'Who is it?' asked Kit, secure in a three-year-old's belief that his mother would know everything.

Andrew looked up at that. 'It's a car,' he said scornfully, and returned to the toy digger that he was pushing through the dust at the bottom of the verandah steps. Like his twin, he was a sturdy little boy, with Hugo's angelic blond hair and her own dark blue eyes, but Juliet knew that the identical looks concealed quite different personalities. Andrew was single-minded, stubborn, happy to play the same game for hours while quicksilver Kit was easily distracted, always asking questions and much more inclined to lead his twin into trouble.

'It is,' Juliet agreed as Kit opened his mouth to object, 'but there's someone in it, so Kit's right too.' She watched the dust cloud moving closer, a slight frown between her brows. 'Perhaps it's the new manager,' she said slowly.

'What's a manager?' That was Kit again, of course, stumbling over the unfamiliar word.

'He's going to help us run the station.'

If there was one thing she needed, it was help, but Juliet couldn't help wondering if she had made the right

5

decision. On the face of it, Cal Jamieson had sounded ideal. 'Cal?' the owner of the neighbouring station had said, when she had rung to ask him for a reference. 'You won't find anyone who knows more about running a property like yours. He's a good man.'

Cal Jamieson might know what he was doing, but whenever Juliet remembered their telephone conversation she was conscious of a faint feeling of disquiet. He had heard that she was looking for a manager, he had said, and he was looking for a job. What was there in that to make her uneasy?

He had sounded brusque, but Juliet had learned not to expect outback men to ooze charm, and in any case Hugo had made her wary of superficial charisma. No, it was something about the way he had taken charge of the conversation. Of course, she had wanted to know that he was competent, but surely it had been up to *her* to suggest that he came out for a trial period? And there had been something more than competence in that deep Australian voice. Looking back, Juliet couldn't pick on any one thing, but she had been left with the uncomfortable feeling that there was a hostile undercurrent to everything he had said.

It was probably just her imagination, Juliet tried to reassure herself. She had never met the man, so what reason could he possibly have to dislike her?

Her eyes rested on the two little boys playing in the dust below her, and, as always, she was conscious of a surge of love so intense that it tightened her throat. Her boys. They were worth every aching bone, every day fighting tears of sheer exhaustion, every sleepless night spent worrying about their future. Wilparilla was their inheritance and she would fight to keep it for them. She didn't care how hostile Cal Jamieson was as long as he helped her to do that.

Still, there was no point in letting him think he could walk all over her. Juliet had no intention of repeating the mistake she had made with the last manager. She would make sure right from the start that Cal Jamieson knew just who was boss!

Pulling off her apron as she went, Juliet went back into the homestead to splash cold water on her face and run her fingers through her dark hair. She grimaced at her reflection in the bathroom mirror. The stress of the last year and the aching exhaustion in her bones had left her looking much older than her twenty-five years and hardly capable of bossing a three-year-old around, let alone a man as tough and self-assured as Cal Jamieson had sounded on the phone. If it came to a contest of vigour, competence and sheer bravado, the much-squeezed tube of toothpaste sitting on the edge of the basin would probably put up a better show than she could at the moment!

For an incongruous moment, she allowed herself to remember the girl she had been in London, so pretty, so vivacious, so certain that everything would work out for the best. That had been before she married Hugo, of course. Now here she was, on an isolated cattle station on the other side of the world, and the only thing she was certain of was that she would do whatever it took to keep Wilparilla safe for her boys. Even if it meant dealing with the unknown Cal Jamieson.

'Mummy, Mummy, the manager's here!' cried Kit, running into the bathroom and bursting to use the new word that he had learnt.

'Well, we'd better go and say hello, then,' said Juliet.

Now that the moment had come, she felt ridiculously nervous. Wilparilla's future rested with the man waiting outside, but she mustn't let him realise how desperately she needed someone to help her.

Kit rushed self-importantly ahead of her onto the verandah and down the steps to find his twin. A man was hunkered down next to Andrew, apparently engaged in serious conversation. All Juliet could see of him as she followed Kit more slowly through the screen door was that he was wearing moleskins and a dark blue shirt. His face was mostly hidden by his hat, but as he turned his head to smile at Kit's eager arrival she caught a glimpse of white teeth beneath the shadow of its brim.

It seemed like such a nice smile that her hopes lifted, but when he glanced up and saw her watching him, it switched off so abruptly that Juliet felt as if she had been slapped. He straightened and took off his hat. 'Mrs Laing?'

Her first impression was of a rangy, quiet-looking man, with a lean face, a cool mouth and cool grey eyes. No, not cool, Juliet corrected herself. Those eyes were cold, icy even, and something in their expression made her want to turn on her heel and bolt back into the homestead.

Mustering a smile from somewhere, she walked down the steps towards him instead. He was even taller than she had thought when she got close to him, and she was conscious of being at a disadvantage as she looked up at him. 'Juliet, please,' she said, and held out her hand. 'You must be Cal Jamieson.'

'Juliet, please,' Cal mimicked her crystal-clear English voice to himself. It sounded just as it had on the telephone, so composed, so self-assured, with that nerve-

grating suggestion of superiority, but otherwise she wasn't at all as he had imagined her. That voice didn't seem to belong to the girl who stood before him.

He hadn't realised that she would be so young. She couldn't be much more than twenty-five, Cal thought, eyeing her unsympathetically. Much too young to own a property like this. A station needed someone who knew the outback, not this girl with her brittle smile and her careful manners.

She was prettier than he had expected, too, Cal admitted grudgingly to himself. Very slender, almost thin, she had dark hair, exquisite cheekbones and wide eyes of so dark a blue they seemed almost purple. He might even have described her as beautiful if it hadn't been for the bruised look about her. There were shadows under her eyes and she held herself warily. She reminded him of a racehorse, skittish and trembling with nerves before a big race. Cal didn't have anything against racehorses, but they didn't belong in the outback. This was brumby country, a place for tough, half-broken horses that could work. They might not be beautiful, but at least they were useful.

Looking at Juliet Laing, Cal doubted if she had ever been of use to anyone other than herself.

'Yes, I'm Cal,' he said in his deep, slow voice, and, because he had little choice, he took her outstretched hand. He had had plenty of time on the long drive from Brisbane to wonder if he was making a terrible mistake coming back to Wilparilla, but now that he had met Juliet for himself he was sure that he had done the right thing after all. This nervy, fragile-looking woman would never last out here. She would run back to England as soon as things got difficult and he would be back where he belonged at long last.

Her handshake was surprisingly firm, though. Cal looked down into her eyes and then wished he hadn't. They were extraordinary eyes, the kind of eyes that could seriously interfere with a man's breathing, and they held besides an expression that gave him pause. There was nothing weak or nervous about the look in Juliet's eyes. It was steady and stubborn.

For a long moment they measured each other, and it seemed to Juliet that an unspoken challenge was issued between them. Quite what the challenge was, she couldn't have said, but she knew that Cal Jamieson thought she didn't belong here. Well, if he thought she was going to turn tail and run, he had another think coming!

'Shall we talk on the verandah?' she asked coolly.

Cal raised his brows. 'Talk?' He made it sound as if she had made an indecent proposal.

'It wasn't much of an interview on the phone,' said Juliet, trying to keep the defensiveness from her voice.

'It's a little late for an interview, isn't it?' said Cal. 'We agreed that I should come for a trial period as manager.'

What did he mean, *we agreed*? thought Juliet crossly. *She* had agreed to employ him on a trial basis.

'I've been driving for the last four days to get here and do just that,' he was saying, unaware of her mental interruption. 'What happens if I don't pass this "interview"? Do you expect me to turn round and go straight back to Brisbane?'

'Of course not.' Juliet set her teeth. This was going to be worse than she had thought. She hadn't been imag-

ining that undercurrent of hostility when she'd spoken
to him on the phone. Not that he was aggressive. No, he
just stood there looking calm and quiet and utterly implacable.

'Look,' she said, making a big effort to sound reasonable, 'Pete Robbins has vouched for you, but all I know
is that you've come from Brisbane and that you need a
job. All you know about me is that I need a manager.
Given that we're going to be working so closely together, I think we should find out a little more about
each other.'

He knew a lot more about her than that, Cal thought
grimly. He knew that she and her husband had come out
from England and bought this place on a whim. He knew
that they'd alienated their neighbours, sacked the experienced stockmen and neglected the property he had
worked so hard to build up, and that now, when her
husband was dead and she had no reason to stay, she
was stubbornly refusing all offers to buy the station from
her. Holding out for more money, he decided in disgust,
as if she didn't have more than enough already. She was
a spoilt, silly woman, and she was in his way.

Cal didn't need to know any more about Juliet than
that, just as she didn't need to know exactly what he was
doing here.

He would humour her for now, Cal thought as he
shrugged an acceptance and followed Juliet up the steps
to the verandah. Let her think that he was desperate for
a job if that was what she wanted.

He sat down in one of the cane chairs and laid his hat
on the floor, glad that Pete Robbins had warned him
about the changes the Laings had made to the old homestead. Hugo Laing's mad scheme had apparently been

the talk of the district. Instead of pouring badly needed money into the property, he had squandered thousands on rebuilding the homestead from scratch. The idea had been to create the kind of luxurious accommodation that would attract a higher class of tourist, but as far as Cal knew no visitor had ever stayed in it.

The stark contrast between the pretentious style of the homestead and the state of the station, crumbling with neglect around it, made Cal angry, but in other ways he was glad. Seeing someone else living in the simple homestead he had shared with Sara would have been hard, and at least now he wouldn't be confronted with the ghosts of the past whenever he came to the house—which wouldn't, he hoped, be that often.

Now Cal looked at Juliet, who had sat on the other side of the cane table. There was an unstudied elegance about her that made her look as if she were posing for a lifestyle spread, in spite of her jeans and simple sand-coloured shirt.

'What kind of things do you want to know?' he asked her.

The bored resignation in his voice grated on Juliet's nerves. He wasn't even *trying* to be pleasant! She had envisaged a casual chat so that they could sum each other up, but Cal made it sound as if she was preparing an interrogation, and, of course, now that they were sitting down, she couldn't think how to begin. She was so tired the whole time that even a simple conversation was beyond her.

'Well, how long have you been in Brisbane, for instance?' she asked at last, horribly conscious of how inane the question sounded.

Cal made no effort to disguise the fact that he thought so too. 'Nearly four years.'

About the same time that she had been out here, Juliet thought. A lifetime. 'What have you been doing there?' she persevered, forcing herself to sound pleasant and relaxed, although something about the way Cal sat there looking completely at home was making her tense. This was *her* home, and he had no right to make it look as if he belonged there and she was the stranger.

Cal hesitated. 'I had my own company,' he said eventually, hoping that she wouldn't ask any more. If she found out how successful it had been, she would wonder what he was doing looking for a job as a manager.

Juliet misinterpreted his hesitation. The company couldn't have been very successful if he was so desperate for a job that he was prepared to come out here and work for her. He obviously didn't want to talk about it, anyway.

'Peter Robbins said that you were originally from this area,' she said instead. 'What made you go to Brisbane in the first place?'

'Personal reasons,' said Cal, taciturn.

'So…er…how do you feel about coming back?'

He stared at her. 'What do you mean, how do I *feel*?'

'I mean, how do you feel?' snapped Juliet. 'Are you happy to be back? Are you sad to leave friends behind in the city? Are you worried about working for a woman?' She sighed. 'You're not very forthcoming, are you?'

What did she think this was, a cocktail party? 'I don't see that it matters,' said Cal, equally exasperated. 'If I were looking for a station manager, I wouldn't waste my time asking him how he felt, I'd want to know what he could *do*. If we have to go through this farce, why don't you try asking me something relevant?'

'I've been trying to find out something about your experience,' said Juliet angrily.

'Experience of what?' he asked with an impatient shrug. 'A station manager's got to be able to do more than sit in an office and manage.'

'OK,' she said, tight-lipped. 'What would you ask, since you seem to know so much about it?'

'If I was employing a manager? I'd want to know if he could fly a plane and drive a road-train. Could he build a dam and fix a generator and sink a bore? Did he understand accounts? And that's before all the obvious stuff like mustering, roping cattle, catching bulls, castrating, branding, dehorning, building fences—'

'All right, all right!' Juliet interrupted him. 'You've made your point. Do I take it you can do all that?' she went on, not without some sarcasm, and he looked her straight in the eye.

'You'll find that out over the next three months, won't you?'

Juliet's dark blue eyes kindled dangerously, and her chin went up as she glared back at him. 'I don't see any point in having a trial at all if your attitude doesn't change,' she said sharply. 'You have made absolutely no effort to be co-operative, or even courteous, since you arrived. Instead you've made it plain that you think I know nothing about running a station.'

Cal opened his mouth, but she swept on before he had a chance to speak. 'Well, that may be true, but one thing I *do* know is that I'm not prepared to pay good money for a manager who's going to talk to me as if I'm stupid! I'm an intelligent woman trying to deal with an extremely difficult situation. I want a manager who can build this station up, run it efficiently and take the time to explain to me what he's doing and why, so that I can learn eventually to run it myself.

'Now, the last manager here couldn't be bothered to do that. He made the mistake of thinking that my opinion didn't count,' Juliet went on grimly, 'so I sacked him.' She fixed Cal with a look, and he was annoyed to find himself noticing how the temper flashing in her eyes had banished that wary, nervous look, leaving her suddenly vivid. Roused out of her brittle poise, she was a force to be reckoned with—and more attractive than he had realised.

'And I'll sack *you,*' she was saying, 'if you forget for one minute that I'm the boss round here. This is my property. I'm prepared to pay whatever it takes for someone to help me, but I'm sure as hell not going to pay to be patronised!'

The expression in Cal's grey eyes was hard to read. If he felt embarrassed or ashamed or intimidated by her outburst, he was certainly giving no sign of it. He wasn't the kind of man she could imagine being intimidated by anything, Juliet thought with an inward sigh.

'I just thought we should know where we stood,' she finished lamely, when Cal didn't say anything. 'It's better to be clear about things from the beginning.'

Cal looked at her. 'The only thing that's clear to me is that you want a manager, a miracle-worker, a slave and a teacher all rolled into one,' he said sardonically. 'I could tell just driving along the track how much work needs to be done here. If I'm going to run this place properly, I won't have time to explain everything to you.'

'I'm not asking for a minute by minute account,' said Juliet. 'I won't be able to spend much time with you with two small children to look after. But I want to know what's going on, and I want to learn what I can.'

'And when you've learnt what you can?'

'Then you'll be out of a job,' she said with a direct look. 'But I'm not a fool. I know how long that will take me, so the job is secure for a while yet, if that's what's worrying you.'

It wasn't security that was worrying Cal, it was the realisation that Juliet Laing was going to be trickier to deal with than he had anticipated. He had expected a spoilt, helpless widow, all ready to be persuaded—in the nicest possible way—that her only option was to sell up and go back to England where she belonged, but the more he looked at Juliet, the less persuadable she seemed. There was a wilful set to that lovely mouth, a stubborn tilt to her chin, a steadiness in the deep blue eyes that was almost unsettling.

Well, he didn't have a reputation for handling difficult horses for nothing, Cal thought. At least he was here, in the best position to influence her to give up and to step forward with the money to buy his station back when she finally accepted the inevitable. He would have to be careful not to antagonise her too much at this stage. It might go against the grain to kow-tow to a woman like Juliet Laing, but she had already sacked one manager, and he wouldn't put it past her to replace him with another man who might be quick to spot the advantages of the situation. Attractive, single women with half a million acres at their disposal weren't that easy to come by. Who was to say some other manager might not decide that he might as well make his position permanent by marrying Juliet and getting a cattle station thrown in as part of the bargain?

Cal's mouth set into a hard line at the thought. He would never get Wilparilla back if that happened. No, he would have to grit his teeth and take Juliet's orders for now, but he would make sure she understood how hopeless her situation was, and with any luck she would soon be gone.

'All right,' he said at last. 'As long as you don't want a detailed report in triplicate every day, I'll let you know what's going on.'

Anyone would think he was doing her a favour! Juliet suppressed a sigh. It was hardly the most gracious acceptance of her terms, but she suspected that it was all she was going to get. 'OK,' she said.

'So, have I passed the interview?' Cal asked, and she stiffened at the sarcastic edge to his voice. She would have loved to have told him to go back to Brisbane, but she was desperate for a manager, and Cal knew it. It could take weeks to find another manager, and she couldn't afford to wait any longer. The station was already falling apart before her eyes as it was. And although he might rub her up the wrong way, there was no denying that he *looked* reassuringly capable and competent. Now he would have to prove it.

'You've passed the interview, yes,' she told him with a cool look. 'We'll see how things work out over the next three months. Needless to say, the trial period we agreed works both ways. If you don't like working for me, you're free to leave whenever you like.'

So she didn't think he'd last the course, did she? Cal smiled grimly to himself as he picked up his hat and got to his feet. Juliet Laing might be tougher than she looked, but they would see who left Wilparilla first!

'Whatever you say,' he drawled, and then added after a pause that made the word sound somehow insulting, 'boss.'

Cal had evidently decided to put an end to the discussion, thought Juliet, vaguely resentful, but as she could hardly order him to sit down again, she stood up too and forced a smile.

'Now we've got over the formalities, would you like a beer?'

He settled his hat on his head. 'I think we'd better go and settle in first.'

'We?' said Juliet idly, thinking that he must have brought his dog with him.

Cal nodded over to the dusty four-wheel drive parked in the shade of a huge gum tree. 'My daughter's with me,' he said.

For a moment Juliet wondered if she had heard right. 'Your *daughter*? You didn't say anything about bringing a daughter!'

'I didn't see what difference it would make to you,' Cal told her, quite unperturbed. He gestured out at the distant horizon. 'It's not as if you don't have the room.'

'But…how old is she?'

'Nine.'

Juliet stared at him. 'You can't bring a nine year-old girl out to a place like this! What about her mother?'

'My wife died six years ago.'

'I'm very sorry,' said Juliet, thrown by the bald statement, 'but it still doesn't seem a very suitable arrangement. Wouldn't she have been better off staying in Brisbane?'

'No,' he said. 'Natalie stays with me.'

Juliet refrained from pointing out that in that case he should have stayed in Brisbane too. 'What were you planning to do with her while you were out during the day?' she asked instead.

'You said yourself that this is just a trial. She can come with me to begin with, and if it works out I'll arrange for my own housekeeper to keep an eye on her while she does her schoolwork. Natalie's a sensible child, she knows what life is like out here.'

'And am I expected to accommodate all these extra people?' Juliet demanded angrily.

If rumour was correct, there were enough rooms in the homestead for three times as many people, but Cal had no intention of staying with her. 'There's a perfectly adequate manager's house,' he said. 'Or so Pete Robbins told me when he said you were looking for a manager,' he added quickly, before Juliet could wonder how he was so well-informed about the accommodation.

'There is a house used by managers in the past,' Juliet agreed, 'but it's in no fit state for a child, and I doubt if you'd get a housekeeper anywhere near it!'

Cal frowned. 'What do you mean? You didn't mention a problem about the house on the phone.'

'That's when I thought you would be on your own. I'm afraid the last manager left it in a terrible state, and I haven't had a chance to go and clear it up. I didn't think you'd mind sleeping in the stockmen's quarters until then, but you can't take a little girl there. Go and see for yourself if you don't believe me,' she said, when Cal looked unconvinced.

'I will,' he said grimly. It had never occurred to him that there would be a problem with the manager's house.

It was small, just two bedrooms, and not what Natalie was used to, but he had only ever thought of it as a temporary measure until Juliet sold him the station and they could move back into the homestead. Now what was he going to do?

'You'd better bring...Natalie, is it?...over,' said Juliet, as if answering his unspoken question. 'She can stay with me while you go and look at the house.'

Cal hesitated, then nodded briefly. 'All right,' he said.

Natalie had short curly brown hair, brown eyes and a shy, solemn face. Juliet smiled at her. 'Hello, Natalie. Welcome to Wilparilla.'

Natalie murmured a shy greeting, and Juliet took her over to meet the twins. 'The grubby one on the left is Kit,' she told the little girl, 'and the even grubbier one beside him is Andrew. They're nearly three.'

'How do you tell them apart?' whispered Natalie, eyes wide as she looked from one to the other, and Juliet smiled.

'I always know which one is which, but it's difficult for everybody else. I make sure they're wearing different clothes, so that makes it easier. Kit's got the blue top on and Andrew's is yellow.' She glanced down at Natalie. 'You must be thirsty after your long drive. Would you like a drink while Dad goes to look at the house?'

Kit scrambled up at that. 'Mummy, my want a drink!'

'Please may I have a drink,' Juliet corrected him automatically.

'Please my want a drink,' said Kit obediently, and Natalie giggled behind her hand as Juliet sighed and settled for that.

'Come on, Andrew, you can have a drink too,' she said and turned to tell Cal how to find the manager's house. But he had ruffled Natalie's hair in farewell and was already striding away. She watched him for a moment, puzzled by the way he seemed to know exactly where he was going, but then shrugged and forgot about it as she ushered the three children through the screen door.

Natalie had lost her shyness entirely with the twins by the time Cal came back. She was sitting at the kitchen table showing them how to blow bubbles in their drinks when he walked into the kitchen. Juliet, leaning by the sink and watching the children indulgently, straightened abruptly as he appeared and her heart gave an odd jump.

Cal was tight-lipped with anger. 'The house is disgusting,' he said furiously, without any preliminaries. 'I wouldn't ask a dog to live in there! How was it allowed to get into that kind of state?'

'I never even went there until last week.' Juliet was immediately on the defensive. 'Hugo—my husband—always dealt with the men.' Not that he had been around to do much dealing, she remembered bitterly, and when he had been there all he had done was set the men's backs up, until all the good ones had left and only the men who didn't care were left at Wilparilla.

'I'm sorry,' she said helplessly, ashamed but tired, too, of apologising for Hugo's mistakes.

Cal took an angry turn around the kitchen. 'Natalie can't stay there,' he said. 'And the men's quarters aren't much better. I checked.'

'That's what I tried to tell you before,' Juliet pointed out. She paused, desperately trying to think of an alternative, but there simply wasn't anywhere else for a child to go. 'Look, I think the best thing you can do is to stay here at the homestead,' she said eventually. 'There are plenty of spare rooms.'

Cal hesitated, raking his fingers through his brown hair in frustration. The last thing he wanted was to be beholden to Juliet Laing, and if it had been just him he would have slept in his swag under the stars, but Natalie couldn't do that. He didn't have any choice, he realised heavily.

'Thank you,' he said with evident reluctance, adding quickly, 'It will just be until we can fix up the house. We'll go as soon as we can.'

CHAPTER TWO

'THERE'S beer in the fridge if you'd like one,' Juliet said rather hesitantly as Cal came in from unloading the car. She knew that the offer sounded rather ungracious, but Cal hadn't been particularly gracious about staying in the homestead. It didn't seem to have occurred to him that she might not be that thrilled at the thought of sharing her home with him either.

If Cal resented her lukewarm tone, he gave no sign of it. Nodding his thanks, he took a bottle from the fridge and pulled off the top. Juliet, preparing vegetables in the sink for the children's supper, tried not to watch him, but her eyes kept sliding sideways to where he stood, leaning casually against the worktop, his head tipped back as he drank thirstily.

She hadn't thought to ask him how old he was, but she guessed that he was in his thirties. He had the toughness and solidity of maturity, but his face wore a guarded expression that made it hard to be sure of anything about him. He could hardly have been more different from Hugo, Juliet reflected. Hugo had been volatile, swinging from breezy charm to sullen rage with bewildering speed. Cal was, by contrast, coolly self-contained. It was impossible to imagine him shouting or waving his arms around wildly. Even the way he stood there and drank his beer suggested an economy of movement, a sort of controlled competence that was at once reassuring and faintly intimidating.

His presence seemed to fill the kitchen, and Juliet was

suddenly, overwhelmingly aware of him as a man: of the muscles working in his throat, of the brown fingers gripped around the bottle, of the dust on his boots and the creases round his eyes and the coiled, quiet strength of his lean body. She couldn't tear her eyes off him. It was as if she had never seen a man before, had never been struck by the sheer physicality of a male body before that moment.

Cal was unaware of her gaze at first. The beer was very cold. To Cal, hot, frustrated and tired after a long day, it tasted like the best beer he had ever had. He lowered the bottle to thank Juliet properly, only to find that she was watching him with a dark, disturbingly blue gaze, and as their eyes met he was conscious of a strange tightening of the air between them, of an unexpected tingling at the base of his spine.

Juliet felt it too. He saw her eyes widen, and a faint flush rose in her cheeks before she turned away and concentrated almost fiercely on peeling a potato.

Oddly shaken by that tiny exchange of glances, Cal levered himself away from the units and, a faint frown between his brows, took his beer over to the table where Natalie was entertaining the twins. She was normally a shy, quiet child, more comfortable with animals than people, but she had obviously taken to the twins immediately, and her face was lit up in a way that he hadn't seen for years now.

Not since they had left Wilparilla, in fact. Cal shook off the unsettling effect Juliet's eyes had had on him and sat down next to his daughter, remembering how she had wept into her pillow and begged to be taken home. He had done the right thing bringing her back, even if things weren't working out quite as he had planned.

'Dad!' Natalie tugged at his sleeve. 'Show Kit and Andrew that trick you do.'

At the sink, Juliet could hear the noise behind her, and she turned, potato in one hand, peeler in the other, to see the twins convulsed with laughter, Natalie giggling and Cal, straight-faced, turning his hand back and forth as if looking for something. 'Again!' shouted Kit, clambering excitedly over Cal as if he had known him all his life.

Juliet's smile was rather twisted as she watched them. At times like these it hurt to realise how much the boys missed in not having a father. Did Cal ache this way when he saw his daughter without a mother?

Natalie seemed a nice little girl. She obviously adored her father, but from what Juliet had seen of him so far she thought he must be a formidable figure for her. He had been dour, if not downright hostile, ever since he had arrived. Not that the children seemed to find him nearly as intimidating as she did, Juliet had to admit. They were still squealing with laughter as he confounded them each time with whatever he was concealing in his hands.

It was then that Cal, unable to keep a straight face any longer, gave in and smiled at the twins' delight, and Juliet nearly dropped her potato. Who would have thought that he could smile like that? Who could have guessed that cool mouth could crease his face with such charm, that the steely look could dissolve into warmth and humour, that the cold grey eyes could crinkle so fascinatingly?

Juliet was disturbed to discover how attractive Cal was when he smiled. She didn't want him to be attractive. Somehow it was easier to think that he was always cold and hostile than to know that he was nice to children, and to wonder why it was that he would never smile at *her* the way he smiled at them.

As if to prove her point, Cal looked up, and his smile faded as he saw the peculiar look on Juliet's face. Probably waiting to point out that she had employed him as a manager, not a children's entertainer, he thought with an edge of bitterness.

He drained his beer and pushed back his chair. 'When do the men finish for the day?' he asked Juliet, ignoring the children's disappointment. If she wanted an efficient manager, that was what he would be.

'About now.' As if suddenly realising that she was still clutching a potato and peeler, Juliet turned back to the sink. Why should she care if he wouldn't smile at her? she asked herself, refusing to admit that she was hurt by the way his attitude changed so completely whenever he looked at her.

'I think I heard the ute go by a few minutes ago,' she added, glad to hear that her own voice sounded just as cool as his. 'They should be back in their quarters by now.'

'How many men are down there?'

'Four at the last count.' Juliet dropped the last potato in the saucepan and filled it with water. 'I haven't had much to do with them. The last manager brought them in when he'd succeeded in getting rid of all the experienced stockmen who were here when we arrived. His wife used to cook for them. I offered to give them meals up here when she left, but they obviously didn't want to sit down with me every evening, so they take it in turns to do their own cooking.'

Juliet tried hard to keep the loneliness and rejection out of her voice. It had been so long since she had had anyone to talk to that she would have welcomed the company of even the dour and taciturn men who so clearly disliked her. 'I only ever see them when one of them comes up to ask for more flour or sugar or whatever. They don't seem to require much in the way of fresh vegetables,' she added with a would-be careless shrug.

Cal frowned as he set the empty bottle on the side. 'Then who tells them what to do every day?'

'No one,' said Juliet bitterly. 'I didn't have much choice but to tell them to carry on with whatever they would normally be doing until the new manager arrived, but I know they thought I was stupid to have sacked the last man in the first place. For all I know they've just been lying around for the last couple of weeks.'

She set the pan on the cooker and turned on the element, then wiped her hands on her apron, trying to make Cal understand. 'I'm pretty much tied to the house with the twins,' she said. 'I can't leave them here on their own, and it's too far to take them with me if I wanted to go and check up on the men—even if I knew where they were and what they were supposed to be doing in the first place.'

'You've been here over three years,' Cal pointed out. What he had seen of Wilparilla so far hadn't left him in any mood for sympathy. He had sold a thriving property and had come back to find that all his hard work had been thrown away and the station left to crumble into disrepair. 'You must have had some idea.'

'My husband never involved me in the station side of things.' Hugo had never involved her in anything, thought Juliet dully. She looked down at her hands, unable to meet Cal's eyes directly. 'When we first came here, he was taken up with the idea of turning Wilparilla into a place that would attract the kind of tourists who want to see the outback but who want a bit of luxury too. There was a nice little homestead here before, but Hugo said it wouldn't be big enough or smart enough, so he knocked it down and built this one.'

Juliet looked around her at the state-of-the-art kitchen, with its view out onto the wide, shady verandah that ran completely round the house. Everything had been done with a designer's style, but it still made her angry to think of how much money Hugo had poured into the house when the station around it was neglected and falling inexorably apart. She had tried to remonstrate with Hugo, but he had brushed her objections aside. It was his money, he had said, and he knew what he was doing.

'I went to Darwin to have the twins in hospital, and I ended up staying there nearly a year while the homestead was being rebuilt. I wanted to come back earlier, but Hugo said I would find it impossible with two babies.'

Juliet stopped as she realised that the bitterness in her voice was telling Cal a little too much about the state of her marriage. 'The point is that I haven't been able to spend the last three years learning about Wilparilla,' she told him. 'Even after I came back, I had my hands full with the twins. They were only just two when Hugo was killed last year. Looking after two toddlers doesn't leave you much time to learn how to run a cattle station.

'Everything's so far away out here,' she sighed. 'It takes so long to get anywhere. There's no toddler group when it takes two hours to get to the nearest town, and no handy babysitter when your neighbours live eighty miles away. I haven't even had the time to make the most basic of social contacts.' The blue eyes were defensive as she looked back at Cal. 'I had no choice but to rely on the manager Hugo had appointed.'

Cal's mouth turned disapprovingly down at the corners. 'Judging by what I've seen so far, he wasn't much of a manager,' he said.

'I know,' snapped Juliet. 'I've got eyes. I only see a tiny fraction of the property, but even that looks run down. But I couldn't do anything about it when Hugo was alive, and when he died...' She trailed off. How could she explain what a terrible financial and emotional mess Hugo had left behind him? 'Well, it wasn't a very good year,' she went on after a moment. 'It was all I could do just to keep things as they were.'

It was the first time Cal had thought what it might have been like for Juliet since her husband's death, and he was conscious of a stirring of shame that he had never considered the matter from her point of view. It couldn't have been easy for her, isolated, and far from home, bringing up two small children alone.

She could have sold, though, he reminded himself. He had offered a good price for the station. She could have gone back to England a rich woman and made things easy on herself, but she hadn't. She had chosen the hard way.

'I'll go and have a word with the men now,' he said, exasperated by the momentary sympathy he had felt for Juliet. 'They're going to start work tomorrow, and they'd better be ready for it.'

'Should I come and introduce you?' Juliet asked doubtfully

'There's no need for that,' said Cal, a grim look about his mouth as he thought about the men who had let his property fall into disrepair. 'I'll introduce myself.'

He didn't say anything about Natalie, so when he had gone Juliet gave her something to eat with the boys. She could hardly leave the child just sitting there, and judging by the way Natalie gobbled it all up she was starving. Afterwards, Natalie helped her wash up, drying each plate with painstaking care.

'You're very well trained, Natalie!' said Juliet, keeping a wary eye on a glass.

'Dad always makes me do chores,' Natalie admitted with something of a sigh. 'I have to dry up and sweep the floor and tidy my bedroom every day.'

'Oh? Is he very strict?'

'Sometimes,' said Natalie. 'And sometimes he's funny. We do good things together.'

Hugo had never wanted to do anything with his sons. 'Does he look after you all by himself?' asked Juliet, uneasily aware that she shouldn't be pumping the child, but, given Cal's uncooperative attitude, it seemed to be the only way she would ever find out anything about him.

'Most of the time,' said Natalie, untroubled by any fine sense of ethics. 'We used to have housekeepers, but they all fell in love with Dad so we don't have them any more. Dad doesn't like it when they do that.'

'I can imagine,' said Juliet dryly. All those housekeepers must have been brave women to fall in love with a man like Cal Jamieson. He wasn't exactly encouraging. But perhaps he had smiled at them...

She pulled herself up short. Was that why Cal was so hostile? she wondered. Was he afraid *she* was going to be tiresome and fall in love with him as well? Juliet felt quite ruffled at the very idea. She had no intention of falling in love again, least of all with a man who patently disliked her and was one of her employees to boot! Love had hurt too much the first time round. Juliet had learnt the hard way how fragile her heart was, and she wasn't going to let it be broken again.

Natalie helped her bathe the twins and put them to bed, and then, when there was still no sign of Cal, Juliet let her choose where she would like to sleep. Puzzled, she watched as Natalie looked in every room, as if expecting to find something. 'Why not have this room next to the twins?' she suggested, when Natalie only looked disappointed. She pointed at the door opposite. 'Dad can sleep across the hall there.'

'OK.'

Juliet made up the bed, and helped her unpack her suitcase. Natalie took out a framed photograph of Cal and a pretty blonde girl holding a toddler on her knee. 'That's Dad, and that's me when I was a baby, and that's Mum,' she said, showing Juliet the picture.

'She was very pretty, wasn't she?' said Juliet, and, when Natalie nodded, added gently, 'Do you miss her?'

Natalie considered. 'I don't remember her very well,' she said honestly. 'But Dad says she was very nice so I think I do.'

She could only have been three when her mother had died—the same age as the twins. Poor Natalie, thought Juliet. Poor Cal.

She wondered again about him as she made up the bed. She didn't know what to make of him. He had seemed so taciturn and hostile at first, but he was so different when he played with the children, and Natalie had made him sound like a different man again. It was odd, Juliet thought idly, how clearly she could picture him already, almost as if she had always known those cool, quiet eyes and that cool, cool mouth.

Smoothing down the bottom sheet, Juliet found herself imagining him lying there, lean and brown and tautly muscled. Her palm tingled, as if she were running her hand over his skin instead, and she swallowed. When

Natalie cried 'Dad!' she spun round as if she had been
caught in the act itself.

'Dad, look, we're making a bed for you!'

'So I see,' said Cal, but his grey eyes rested on Juliet's
flushed face, and he raised one eyebrow at her guilty
expression. She was sure that he could see exactly what
she had been thinking about.

'We...I just thought... since you weren't here...'
Juliet realised that she was floundering and forced herself to stop. This was her house and she had a perfect
right to be here. She didn't have to explain anything to
anyone, least of all to Cal, who was (a) her employee,
and (b) late.

'It's very kind of you,' said Cal coldly, 'but there was
no need. I'll finish it off.'

Juliet felt dismissed. 'I've...er, I wasn't sure what you
wanted to do about eating, but I've made supper if you'd
like to eat later,' she said awkwardly.

'Thank you.'

He didn't say 'you may go', but that was what it felt
like. He stepped out of the doorway and Juliet sidled
past him and slunk back down to the kitchen. Behind
her, she could hear Natalie excitedly telling him about
Kit's bedtime story, and how Andrew had splashed in
the bath, and she felt a great wash of loneliness sweep
through her. She had no one to tell about her day. How
long was it since she had had anyone to talk to in the
evenings?

A long time.

She had hoped that she would have been able to make
some friends amongst her neighbours after Hugo had
died, but everyone lived so far away, and she soon discovered that he had left her a legacy of distrust and
disapproval. On the few occasions she had made the la-

borious journey to the nearest town, her attempts to be
friendly had been met with politeness but no warmth,
and she had been too tired and depressed to persevere.
Rebuffed, she had retreated into herself, and relied on
letters and phone calls to friends in England for support
instead. She had told herself that she wasn't lonely as
long as she had the twins, but she had been.

In an effort to cheer herself up, Juliet showered and
changed into a cool cotton dress. She had bought it in
London years ago, and the deep turquoise colour always
made her feel more positive. Kit and Andrew were
happy and healthy, she reminded herself, and with Cal
as manager she had taken the first step towards saving
Wilparilla. That was what mattered.

Her equilibrium restored, she made her way back to
the kitchen, where she found Cal looking out through
the windows towards the creek. He swung round at the
sound of her footsteps and stared at her. Juliet had the
oddest feeling that he had forgotten her existence until
that moment.

Cal was, in fact, thrown more than he wanted to admit
by the sight of Juliet standing in the doorway. The
kitchen had been very quiet when he had come in, and
he had been standing there, remembering the simple
room it been before all the polished wood and gleaming
chrome. He had spent long, long evenings alone in here
after Sara had died, while Natalie slept down the corridor, torn between his instinct to stay at Wilparilla and
the promise he had made to his dead wife.

Now, suddenly, he was no longer alone, and Juliet
was there, warm and vibrant in a blue dress, but with
that wary look on her face. Irrelevantly, he found himself
wondering what she would look like if she relaxed and
smiled for a change.

He lifted his hand to show the bottle. 'I helped myself to a beer. I hope you don't mind.' He thought his voice sounded odd, but Juliet didn't seem to notice anything wrong.

'Of course not,' she said, very formal.

There was a pause. 'Is Natalie in bed?' she asked at last, and Cal nodded.

'She's tired. It's been a long journey for her.' He hesitated. 'Thank you for looking after her. She seems to have had a good time.'

'She was very helpful,' said Juliet. 'She's a nice little girl.' She would have liked to ask about Natalie's schooling. Presumably she would do her lessons with the School of the Air. But Juliet suspected that Cal would interpret any questions as criticism, and, since they seemed to be being polite to each other for now, it was a shame to spoil it.

Instead, she went over to the oven and took out the supper. 'How did you get on with the men?' she asked as she set it on the table.

Cal pulled out a chair and sat down. 'I think they know who's boss now,' he said, grimly remembering the scene in the stockmen's quarters. He had been down to the stockyards before he went to see them, and had been so angry at the way everything had been neglected and allowed to fall into disrepair that he had been in no mood to make allowances.

'And who *is* boss?' enquired Juliet in a frosty voice as she took a seat opposite him.

'As far as they're concerned, I am. As far as I'm concerned, you are.' Cal met her look evenly. 'Is that a problem?'

'Why is it so hard for them to accept that this is my

property?' she asked, disgruntled. 'Is it because I'm a woman? Because I'm English?'

'It's because you don't know anything about running a cattle station,' said Cal flatly. 'You admitted as much yourself. Yes, you've got a bit of paper that says you own Wilparilla, but these men aren't interested in that.'

He nodded his head in the direction of the stockmen's quarters. 'They're only going to work if they know that the person giving them orders understands what they're doing, and in this case that's me. Now, you can go down and give them a little lecture on property rights if you like, but you're paying me to get them organised and get some work done on this station again, and I'll only be able to do that if they think of *me* as boss for the time being. If you're not happy with that, you'd better say so now.'

'I don't have very much choice but to be happy with it, do I?' said Juliet a little bitterly.

Cal just shook his head in exasperation and applied himself to his meal. In a way, he was glad she was being unreasonable. It was much easier to find her irritating, to remember how perversely she was standing in way of all he wanted, than to notice how smooth and warm her skin looked, how her dark hair gleamed in light, how even when her lips were pressed together in a cross line, like now, her mouth hinted at a fiery, passionate nature beneath that brittle cool.

Why was she so obsessed about being boss anyway? She had no idea about Wilparilla. She didn't know the land. She didn't know the creeks and gullies the way he did. She had never ridden all day through the heat and the dust, or slept out under the stars while the cattle shifted their feet restlessly in the darkness.

She would never be the boss of Wilparilla, Cal vowed

to himself. She didn't belong on a cattle station. All she knew was this homestead. She probably wouldn't even recognise a cow if she saw one, he thought contemptuously. Look at her! Sitting there like some exotic bird that had lost its way and found itself in the desert instead of the hot-house environment where it belonged. What was the point of wearing a dress that curved over her breast like that? A dress that let him glimpse the hollows at the base of her throat and made him wonder about the soft material whispering over her skin as she moved?

'You don't like me, do you?' His face didn't give much away, but Juliet could feel his dislike as clearly as if he had stood up and shouted it.

Cal took a pull of his beer and looked across the table at her. He might have known she would prove to be one of those women who wanted to be up front about their feelings. No, he didn't like her, but he was damned if he was going to indulge her by admitting it. She would only start asking 'why not?' and before they knew what had happened they would be picking over emotions as if any of it mattered.

On the other hand, why should he make things easy for her by denying it? 'I don't think this is the right place for you,' he temporised at last.

'Why not?'

He had known *that* was coming! 'I would have thought it was obvious,' he said, irritated at having fallen into the same old trap. Why did women always have to know the reason? Why couldn't they just accept things for what they were?

'Not to me,' said Juliet, who had hoped to put Cal out of countenance and was annoyed to find that he didn't even have the grace to look embarrassed at being confronted with his hostility.

Cal sighed. Well, if she was so anxious to know what he thought, he would tell her. 'This is a working cattle station. Life out here is rough and dirty. It's not a place where you put on a pretty dress and pretend you'll never have to get mud under your fingernails.'

'You've had a shower and changed your clothes,' Juliet pointed out, dangerously sweet.

'Yes, but not into the kind of clothes I'd wear to a smart restaurant.'

'So I'm not allowed to wear anything but torn jeans and a checked shirt, is that it?'

Cal looked impatient. 'It's not a question of *allowing*,' he said irritably. 'I'm just saying that you're not wearing the right clothes if you want to belong.'

'But I do belong,' said Juliet, pushing her plate aside. 'This is my house,' she told him deliberately, 'and I can wear whatever I like in it. I advise you not to forget that.'

The haughty note in her voice made Cal's lips tighten. It was almost as if she knew how much he hated her reminding him that Wilparilla belonged to her, and was taunting him deliberately. Yes, it had been his choice to sell, but the Laings hadn't cared for the land. He was the one who had built Wilparilla up into a successful station, and in Cal's heart it was still his.

Across the table, his eyes met Juliet's challenging gaze. 'I don't think there's much chance of me forgetting that,' he said, and his voice was very cold.

They finished the meal in silence, constrained on Juliet's part, apparently unconcerned on his. Afterwards, she had half expected him to make his excuses and leave, but instead he found a tea-towel and without being asked began to dry the dishes as she washed up.

It was strange for Juliet to have someone to help. She

wasn't used to anyone else being with her in the kitchen.
Few people came out to the station, and anyone with
business on the station had eaten with the manager and
stayed in the stockmen's quarters. It was certainly
quicker with Cal there, but Juliet half wished that he had
left her to do it on her own. She was very aware of him
standing beside her, not saying anything, looking
through the window at the darkness, absorbed in his own
thoughts, not caring if she was there or not. Out of the
corner of her eye, she could see his hands moving, un-
hurried and competent, and she found herself watching
them as if fascinated. They were brown and strong, and
there were fine golden hairs at his wrist.

He wasn't handsome, Juliet told herself. Not handsome in the way Hugo had been, anyway. Really, he
was quite ordinary. Brown hair, grey eyes, nothing special.

There was something implacable about him, though.
Something hard and strong and steady. A quiet coldness
that mesmerised and unnerved her at the same time.
Beneath her lashes, Juliet's eyes rested on his mouth.
That wasn't the mouth of a cold man, she found herself
thinking, and she remembered how he had smiled at the
twins. The memory snaked down her spine, and something shifted deep inside her so that she jerked her gaze
away.

She tried to concentrate on how obvious he had made
his distaste, but all she could think about was him lying
in the bed she had made, his long brown body bare
against the cool sheet. She could imagine it so clearly
that she sucked in her breath, and the tiny sound made
Cal turn his head to find her eyes wide and dark
and startled, as if she had just thought of something
shocking.

'What is it?' he asked.

'Nothing.' Juliet's fingers trembled as she pulled out the plug and made a big deal of rinsing out the sink. She had to get a grip of herself! 'That is…' She stopped. No, that wasn't a good idea.

'What?'

'It doesn't matter.'

Cal frowned irritably. If she had something to say, why didn't she get on with it? 'What doesn't?'

Driven into a corner, Juliet wiped her hands on a tea-towel and wished she had never opened her mouth. But Cal obviously wasn't going to let it drop, and maybe it needed saying after all.

'I was just thinking that it might be a good idea if we established a few ground rules.' She pushed her hair behind her ears, absurdly nervous for some reason.

He looked at her with that infuriatingly unreadable expression. 'Ground rules?'

'Yes. I mean, we're going to be living together until we can get the manager's house cleaned up, so perhaps we should agree a few things now.'

'What sort of things?'

'Well,' she said, 'I presume you don't want to cook separately, so we need to decide about meals, that kind of thing and…well, you know…how we ensure that we both have some privacy,' she finished lamely. It had seemed so sensible when she started, but under Cal's dispassionate gaze she found herself faltering for some reason.

'You're very keen on rules, aren't you?' he said sardonically, and she flushed and lifted her chin.

'Sometimes they save awkwardness.'

'I don't see what's awkward about sharing a few meals.'

'I didn't just mean that,' said Juliet. 'I meant the situation generally.'

'What *situation*?' asked Cal, exasperated.

'You know what I mean!' she flared. He was being deliberately obtuse! 'The fact is that the two of us will be alone together here for much of the time.'

'Ah!' he exclaimed, suddenly enlightened—as if he hadn't known all along exactly what she was talking about, Juliet thought sourly. 'You want some rules to make sure I don't take advantage of you, is that it?'

'Yes...*no*!' she corrected herself frantically as Cal raised an eyebrow. 'Of course not,' she said more calmly. 'All I'm trying to say is that we're both adults, both single. If we don't acknowledge that now, I can see a situation arising where we might...might...' She could feel herself floundering again and wished she'd never opened her mouth. 'Well, we might...might *wonder*...'

'Might wonder what it would be like if I kissed you?' Cal suggested in a hatefully calm voice, but she was too relieved to have the sentence completed for her to resent him.

'That kind of thing, yes.'

She was standing by the cooker in her turquoise dress, hugging her arms together self-consciously and wearing a defensive expression that made her look very young. Cal looked at her thoughtfully for a moment, then laid his tea-towel over the back of a chair.

'Let's find out now,' he said, coming over to Juliet.

She looked at him blankly. 'Find what out?'

'What it would be like if I kissed you.' He took her hands and unfolded her arms so impersonally that he had taken hold of her waist before Juliet had quite realised what was happening. 'Then we won't need to wonder,' he explained briskly, drawing her towards him, 'and we won't need any rules.'

And with that he bent his head and kissed her.

Juliet's hands came up quite instinctively to clutch at the sleeves above his elbows for support as his mouth came down on hers and the floor seemed to drop away beneath her feet.

It was a hard, punishing kiss, a kiss meant to teach her a lesson. Juliet knew that, but she was unprepared for the searing response that shot through her at the feel of his lips and his hands hard against her. It seemed to leap into life, jolting between them like electricity, at once shocking and dangerously exciting, so that the kiss which Cal had intended to be so brief somehow took on a life of its own and he tightened his arms around Juliet, moulding her against him as her lips parted beneath his.

Cal slid one hand up to the nape of her neck, tangling his fingers in the silky hair. He had forgotten how she exasperated him, forgotten her stupid rules, forgotten everything but how warm and soft and pliant she felt in his arms. Caught off-guard by the piercing sweetness of her response, Cal was in the middle of gathering her closer and deepening his kiss when the realisation of just how close they both were to losing control stopped him in his tracks as effectively as a bucket of cold water.

Literally dropping Juliet back to earth, he stepped away from her and took a deep, steadying breath. Juliet was left to collapse back against the cooker, dazed and trembling. They stared at each other for a long, long moment.

'Well, now we know,' said Cal, when he could speak. 'We won't need to waste any more time wondering about it, will we?' He could see Juliet's mouth shaking, and the temptation to pull her back into his arms and forget everything else once more was so strong that he had to make himself turn away.

Juliet was still leaning against the cooker when he reached the door. 'Thanks for the meal', he said, and then he was gone.

CHAPTER THREE

'DAD'S gone to have breakfast with the stockmen,' Natalie announced when Juliet found her in the kitchen the next morning. 'He said to tell you he won't be back until this evening.'

'When did he tell you this?' asked Juliet, put out to discover that all the effort spent on steeling herself to face Cal with cool composure this morning had been completely wasted.

It had taken her ages dithering around in the corridor before she had got up the nerve to even open the kitchen door, and now he had just swanned off for the day without so much as a by-your-leave, leaving a casual message that he would be back later. No doubt she would be expected to have a meal waiting for him when he deigned to turn up, too!

'Just now,' said Natalie. 'He only left a minute ago.' She was anxious to help. 'Shall I go and find him for you?' she offered, halfway off her chair.

'No!' said Juliet quickly. She wasn't up to a confrontation with Cal just yet. 'I mean, no, it doesn't matter, thanks,' she added more gently.

Running her fingers through her hair in a weary gesture, she put on the kettle to make herself some tea. The twins were still asleep. Typical that the one morning she could have had a lie-in she had woken early, feeling hot and cross after a restless night.

It was Cal's fault, of course. Why had he kissed her like that? How could she have let herself be kissed like that? Juliet had lain awake for hours, tossing fretfully from side to side, her heart still pumping at the feel of Cal's hands on her bare arms, her lips still tingling with the touch of his mouth. She'd wanted to be angry with Cal—she *was* angry with him— but deep in her heart she'd known that he wasn't entirely to blame. She hadn't even *tried* to push him away.

It hadn't even been that much of a kiss, she'd tried telling herself. Cal had been making a point, no more than that, but her own electric response had alarmed and shamed her.

She had been alone too long, that was all, Juliet had decided at last in the small hours. It was the only thing that could explain her own bizarre reaction to the way he had kissed her. If it hadn't been for those long months of rejection by Hugo she would never have kissed Cal back as she had. She wouldn't have wanted the kiss to go on and on, and she wouldn't have felt so bereft when he'd let her go.

And she wouldn't have been lying there, squirming with frustration, unable to stop wondering what would have happened if Cal *hadn't* dropped her when he had. He would have been lying in bed, his body where her hand smoothed over the sheet. Juliet's palms had twitched at the thought. She'd felt as if her nerves were jumping just beneath her skin. She'd wished she could stop thinking about what it would be like to touch him, to taste him, to shiver at his hands drifting over her, at his hardness covering her...

She had to stop this!

If Cal thought she was going to make a big deal out of one crummy kiss, he would be disappointed. Juliet had spent too long coping with Hugo's sudden whims and changes of mood. *She* was in charge now, she reminded herself, and she wasn't going to go to pieces just because some man had kissed her.

No, she had hired Cal to manage the station. He would just have to accept that she was his employer, not a convenient diversion for the empty outback evenings.

'Sorry?' Juliet suddenly realised that Natalie was talking to her and that she hadn't heard a word. 'What did you say?'

'I said, the kettle's boiled,' said Natalie, evidently puzzled by Juliet's abstracted air.

As she drank her tea, Juliet wondered whether Natalie was upset at being abandoned by her father for the day, but she seemed to take it in her stride. She was happy to stay with Juliet and the twins, she told Juliet, adding conscientiously, 'If you don't mind.'

The only thing Juliet minded was the way Cal had simply assumed she would be there to look after his daughter, but she could hardly say that to Natalie, and anyway, the little girl turned out to be very useful. It was much easier to get things done knowing that she was keeping an eye on the twins, who were liable to get into all sorts of mischief if they weren't watched like a hawk.

And Juliet had to admit that it was nice to have someone to talk to. It was just a pity that Cal wasn't as open and friendly as his daughter.

Later that afternoon, when the heat of the day began to cool, Juliet took Natalie and the boys down to the paddock to see the horses that were corralled there, waiting their turn to be taken out on a muster, or ridden through the scrub and termite hills where even four-wheel drives couldn't go.

Natalie's eyes shone as she hung over the rail. 'Dad's

going to get me a horse of my own, so I can go riding with him,' she told Juliet proudly.

Juliet patted the neck of a roan that had come in search of a titbit. 'I'd like to get a couple of small ponies for the boys to learn on,' she said.

The twins had always loved watching the horses. They were standing on the rail next to Natalie, not at all afraid of the big mare tossing her head up and down. 'The trouble is that I can't leave one while I teach the other to ride, and I can't control two ponies at once,' she went on, half to herself. She had tried to work out a way round the difficulty many times since the boys had been old enough to walk, but the fact remained that she couldn't teach two small boys to ride at the same time with only one pair of hands.

'Dad could help you,' Natalie offered, and Juliet smiled wryly.

'I think Dad's got more important things to do at the moment.'

'He certainly has.' Cal had come up behind them so quietly that when he spoke, Juliet jumped a mile. The man must move like a cat!

'Where did you come from?' she demanded, heart hammering. It was the shock, she told herself. Nothing to do with the sight of him, lean and strong and somehow immediate in the sharp outback light. Beneath his hat, his eyes were as cool and as impersonal as ever and his mouth—that mouth that she remembered so well from last night—was compressed in an angry line.

'The stockyards,' he said with an edge of impatience. What did it matter where he had come from? It wasn't his fault she had nothing better to do than spend the afternoon leaning on the paddock rail and was so busy looking elegant in khaki trousers and a cream shirt that she hadn't heard him coming.

He turned to Natalie. 'Nat, why don't you take the twins back to the homestead?' he said. 'I need a word with Mrs Laing.'

'I call her Juliet,' said Natalie, but she climbed off the rail.

Juliet bridled at the way Cal was ordering her sons around, but she didn't want to start arguing in front of the children. 'Yes, would you mind getting them a drink, Natalie?' she said tightly. '*I* want to talk to your father.'

She watched Natalie lead Kit and Andrew out of earshot, holding carefully onto two sticky hands, before rounding on Cal. 'I'd be grateful if you'd let *me* decide where and when we talk!' she hissed. 'You're here to manage the station and nothing else. You can leave my children to me!'

'I'm not going to get anything done if I have to spend my time making an appointment to see you,' Cal pointed out, grey eyes cold and contemptuous.

'I'm not asking you to make an appointment! I just object to the way you march in and start ordering everyone around!'

He gave an exasperated sigh. 'I merely suggested that Natalie kept an eye on the boys while we talked. I've got something important to say, and I assumed you'd want to concentrate. You can't do that while you're keeping half an eye on what the children are doing.'

'Couldn't whatever it is you've got to say wait until the children are in bed?' she demanded, and his eyes narrowed.

'No. You've got a big problem here, bigger than I think you realise, and I'm damned if I'm going to hang around and present it to you when you're all primped and perfumed for the evening, just so that you can make a point about being the boss!'

Angry as he was, Cal missed the warning blaze in the dark blue eyes. 'What exactly is the problem?' she asked in a biting voice.

'Everything,' he said bluntly. He was white about the mouth with fury and despair at what had become of Wilparilla since Juliet and her husband had taken over. 'I'll need the plane to get an idea of what's going on in the farthest areas, but from what I've seen today there are enough problems to be going on with in the near paddocks. Fences are down, the watering points are a mess, pipes are broken, the cattle are running wild, most of them haven't even been branded...the whole station is falling apart!'

When he thought of the years of back-breaking work he had put into building up a prime herd and turning Wilparilla into a thriving station, Cal wanted to hit something. He had been edgy and irritable even before he'd set out, conscious of an unsettling sense of guilt about kissing Juliet, and his temper hadn't been improved by the way the memory of how she had felt in his arms seemed to have lodged itself in his brain.

He had tried to shake it off, he'd even thought he had succeeded, and then at odd moments during the day, when he'd least expected it, he would find himself thinking about her fragrance, the silkiness of her hair between his fingers, the way her body had melded into his. The memories disconcerted and distracted him, and he grew increasingly angry, with himself but mostly with Juliet, and by the time the full extent of the Laings' neglect of his land had hit home, he had convinced himself that he hated her.

And now she was standing there, looking appalled, as if she hadn't known how bad things were already!

Cal wanted to hurt her, to make her realise just what she and her husband had done to Wilparilla. He went on, reeling off the problems that had to be faced, the repairs that had to be carried out, the impossible that had to be achieved before the wet season set in, while Juliet seemed to buckle beneath the weight of the difficulties facing her.

Perversely, her stricken expression only made Cal angrier, and he carried on, lashing her with his tongue until Juliet couldn't endure to hear any more and covered her ears with her hands.

Cal snatched them away. 'That won't help!' he raged. 'None of this will go away because you don't want to hear about it! You're so keen to be the boss? That means *you* take responsibility for this mess! It's time someone did,' he added cruelly. 'You should be ashamed of yourself, letting good land fall into this state. Wilparilla could be making a profit, but you've let it run down to the point where you're staring at ruin.'

'It's not that bad,' whispered Juliet. She knew that it was, of course, but she hadn't wanted to accept how close she was to losing Wilparilla for the boys.

'It *is* that bad!' shouted Cal in bitter frustration. 'Oh, I can see why you don't want to accept it, of course,' he went on, deliberately insulting. 'That might mean you'd have to face up to reality instead of sitting around the homestead all day, worrying about what to wear in the evening. The only problem you face up to is how to get everyone to call you boss!'

'How dare you?' Too tired to be able to cope with a single extra problem, let alone the terrifying list Cal had harangued her with, Juliet had been close to tears of despair, but his accusation was so unfair that she was suddenly, gloriously angry.

'Have you ever tried looking after two boys under three?' she shouted back at him. 'Of course you haven't! If you had, you'd know that *you* get more chance to sit down during the day than I do, and if I *did* get a chance, I'd have to spend it trying to sort out the mess of paperwork in the office, or growing enough vegetables to keep us self-sufficient, or ordering supplies, or paying wages to men who don't do any work, and that's before I even *start* thinking about cooking or cleaning or washing clothes.

'And in case it's slipped your mind,' she swept on furiously, 'today I not only had my own children to look after, I also had yours! You just walked out and left her.'

'She's all right—' Cal began, but Juliet wasn't about to let him finish.

'She's *nine*!' she said, her voice as contemptuous as Cal's had been earlier. 'She needs food and drink and attention, just like any other child, and that's what I gave her. Or was I supposed to ignore her and rush around after you all day, letting myself be blamed instead?'

Cal's hands were clenched with rage and a muscle was pounding in his jaw. 'No, but—'

'But nothing!' Juliet interrupted him. 'You obviously have different priorities, but I put the children first. I have to look after them before I can look after the station. I *know* there's a serious problem, and I also know that the only way I can deal with it effectively is to hire a competent manager.

'That's why you're here,' she reminded him in any icy voice. 'If I could do it myself I would, but I can't, so I'm paying *you* to sort out the problem. I'm not paying you to criticise me. Don't you ever—*ever!*—talk to me like that again! If you can't do the job, then you'd better say so, and I'll get in someone else who can do it, and can do it without shouting and insulting me!'

And with that she turned on her heel and stalked off towards the homestead, leaving Cal to slam his hand against the rail post in fury and frustration. He swore out loud. Damn the woman! It would serve her right if he did leave her to sort out the mess on her own! She would be ruined within weeks!

For a moment Cal savoured the thought of telling Juliet just what she could do with her job, but he knew that he couldn't risk it. He could call her bluff, but he wouldn't put it past that dark-eyed witch to let him go and then find some other fool she could boss around to her heart's content.

Cal wished he knew how much money Juliet had behind her. The state of the station suggested that it wasn't much, but it might just mean that she and her husband hadn't been prepared to spend any on improvements and maintenance. He had heard the Laings had vast property interests around the world, so all Juliet would have to do was call her in-laws if she ran short of cash. And even if money *was* a problem, and she went bankrupt, the banks would get involved and it could be months if not years before he could buy Wilparilla back.

No, he would have to stick with it, Cal decided reluctantly. He would stay and toe the line, but he was damned if he was going to save the station for her. He would do the minimum, even if it meant watching Wilparilla degenerate further, until she was forced to admit that she couldn't keep it going any longer.

It wouldn't be long, he vowed.

Juliet herself was still rigid with anger. Somehow she managed to feed the children, but only she knew what it cost her to keep smiling and acting as normal while inside she was screaming with rage and frustration and utter despair.

Cal hadn't needed to be quite so brutal to make her realise how desperate the situation was. The bare facts were enough to terrify her. The prospect of losing Wilparilla pressed down on Juliet. She couldn't give in, she *wouldn't* give in…but what was she going to do?

At least when the children were in bed she could stop smiling. Supper was eaten in glacial silence. As soon as it was over, Cal excused himself, and Juliet was left to do the washing up alone. Even a repetition of last night's kiss would have been better than being alone with her thoughts, Juliet realised wearily, as she stood at the sink, washing dishes like a zombie.

Sometimes it seemed as if she had spent the last few years clambering over an obstacle course, each obstacle higher and harder than the last. Then Hugo had died and she had hoped that she would at least be able to have some control over her life again. She had made the decision to sack the manager and bring in Cal, but that had only replaced one problem with another.

Juliet could have coped with Cal's attitude, but the scale of the problems he had identified terrified her. She didn't know where to begin solving them. All she knew was that if she didn't, the twins would lose the only thing that Hugo had ever given them. Somehow she had to find a way to raise the money to cover the most immediate repairs, but—

Juliet's thoughts broke off as a plate that she was drying mechanically slipped between her hands and smashed onto the floor. She stared down at the mess, her bottom lip trembling with reaction. It felt like the last straw, and she was submerged by a tide of exhaustion and depression so profound that the simple task of clearing it up seemed insuperable.

She did sweep up the pieces in the end, but the effort of doing it without bursting into tears was enormous. Her hands were shaking as she tipped the last of the shards down the rubbish chute. Leaving the rest of the dishes to dry themselves, she dragged herself along the corridor to bed, where she fell like a stone into an exhausted sleep.

The sound of crying dragged Juliet out of the depths in the middle of the night. It's one of the twins, her brain insisted. Get out of bed, it ordered. But her body refused to obey. She lay on the bed as if she were tied down by lead weights. It took an immense effort of will just to open her eyes, but somehow she got her legs to the floor.

By the time she got next door, both boys were awake, both screaming, feeding off the other's distress. Still disorientated, Juliet hung on the door, not knowing which to go to first. In the end, she had to lift Kit over to Andrew's bed so that she could sit and hold them both. She tried to soothe them, but they could sense that she was close to tears of exhaustion and despair herself, and, picking up on her tension, they redoubled their cries.

Further down the corridor, Cal could hear their screams. Let Juliet handle it, he thought. The bloody woman would only resent his interference if he tried to help. No doubt he would be accused of trying to exceed his responsibilities! In any case, it wasn't his fault if she couldn't cope on her own. There was nothing to stop her going home.

He turned on his side, hunching a shoulder irritably, but the cries went on and on, until he could stand it no longer. They would wake Natalie up next. Exasperated, Cal pulled on some shorts and strode down to the twins' room.

The light from the corridor spilled into the room, and he could see Juliet in a white cotton nightdress, sitting on one of the beds and struggling to keep hold of the boys, who were arching back over her arms in a frenzy, their faces screwed up and their little fists clenched as they screamed.

She looked up as he appeared in the doorway, her expression naked with desperation. Without a word, Cal went over and took Andrew from her. He walked the child around the room as if he were a tiny baby, calming him with the security of his hold and the steadiness of his heartbeat. Andrew's head was buried into his shoulder, but as his sobs began to lessen, Cal looked over to see that Juliet's undivided attention had magically soothed Kit too. She held him on her lap while the screams reduced to sobs, and then to little hiccuping gasps, and finally, blissfully, silence.

'What was the matter?' Cal asked in an undertone.

'I don't know.' Her voice was dull with exhaustion, and she looked beaten. 'A nightmare, perhaps. One of them woke up crying, and I didn't get here soon enough to stop him waking the other with a fright.'

Cal craned his head down to look at Andrew's face. His eyes were drooping and his body had gone limp. 'I think they'll sleep now,' he said.

'Yes.' Juliet roused herself to lift Kit from her lap and lay him back down in the bed. As Cal had said, he was almost asleep. Then she took Andrew back and put him down. He murmured something as she bent to kiss him, his little fingers stretching and curling subconsciously.

'You can leave them now,' whispered Cal, and she

realised that she was just standing there, staring down at her son.

She followed Cal to the door like an automaton, and stood blinking in the light. 'I'm sorry,' she said, not looking at him. 'I couldn't stop them crying. I tried, but they wouldn't stop, and I couldn't…I couldn't…'

To her horror, she could hear as if from a distance her voice breaking on the edge of hysteria. She made as if to stumble back to her room, but Cal had her arm in a firm grip.

'Come on,' he said, and propelled her out onto the verandah, pushing her down into a chair. 'Sit there and I'll go and make you some tea.'

Juliet's mouth was working uncontrollably, and she covered her face with her hands. The unexpected gentleness in his voice was more than she could bear. If he had been brusque, she might have pulled herself together, but as it was she broke down and wept in a way she had never allowed herself to weep before.

Cal hesitated. She looked so distraught that he wanted to gather her into his arms and comfort her the way he had comforted Andrew, but she wasn't a child, she was a woman, and he didn't think holding her would be a very good idea.

Nor would Juliet want it. She was his boss, as she kept reminding him, and hired men didn't gather their bosses onto their laps and hold them while they cried, did they?

He turned away, and went to make the tea.

'Here, drink this,' he said when he came back, thrusting a hot mug into her hand. 'It'll make you feel better.'

Juliet clutched the mug in one hand and tried to wipe

her cheeks. 'I'm sorry,' she said on a shuddering breath. 'I don't know why I'm crying like this.'

'Don't you?'

She took a sip of the tea. It was hot and sweet and steadying. 'I'm just so tired,' she admitted on a long sigh. 'Everything's gone wrong, and I've been trying to cope, but it never seems to get any easier, and tonight I couldn't even stop my children crying. I was just sitting there while they were screaming and there was nothing I could do.' Her mouth twisted bitterly at the memory of her own inadequacy. She linked her fingers around the mug and cradled it against her chest.

'If you hadn't come along, we'd probably still be there,' she said, and glanced at Cal. He was leaning forward in his chair, resting his arms on his thighs and holding his own mug loosely between his knees. He wasn't looking at her. He was looking out at the night. The stars were splashed across the great dark bowl of the sky, their light so bright that Juliet could see the silhouettes of the coolabah trees on the way down to the creek.

'Thank you for your help,' she said quietly, almost shyly. 'I didn't realise you would be so good with small children.'

He looked at her then, just once, and then away. 'Sara died when Natalie was three,' he said. 'I know what it's like to have to cope on your own.'

Juliet glanced at him. 'Yes, I suppose you do,' she sighed, although she couldn't imagine him ever being reduced to hysterical tears, ever feeling lonely or afraid or overwhelmed by panic. He seemed too solid, too steady, too capable. But perhaps that was unfair? How would *she* know how he had felt when his wife had died?

They were silent for a while, sipping their tea in the light striping the verandah from the corridor through the wire mesh of the screen door. Juliet rubbed her face absently with the back of her hand. That awful, hysterical feeling had faded and she felt oddly calm, sitting out here with Cal, listening to the sounds of the night.

'I'm sorry about that argument this afternoon,' she said at last.

'So am I,' Cal found himself saying. 'I shouldn't have spoken to you like that.'

'You were right to be angry. I know I have to do something to save Wilparilla, but I don't know where to start.' She swallowed painfully. 'Hugo lost interest in the station long ago. They hadn't even finished building the house before he got bored with the tourist idea and started spending time in Sydney again. When I got back here, nothing was happening on the station. All the men who'd been working here when he first bought the property had left, and he'd brought in a manager who didn't seem to care any more than he did.'

Juliet sighed. 'I thought, when Hugo was killed in that car accident, that at least I could do something about getting things going again, but the manager wasn't going to help me. I didn't have much choice but to stick out the wet season, and then I'd hoped that we could make a fresh start together, but all he would do was tell me that I should sell up.'

Cal grimaced to himself. 'Why didn't you?' he said, studying her over the rim of his mug. 'It's hard enough to bring up two small children on your own without having the worry of a station like this to run.'

'Because Wilparilla is all Kit and Andrew have,' said Juliet, her eyes on the black outlines of the trees against the black night. 'Hugo wasn't interested in his children,' she went on with difficulty. 'He couldn't even be bothered to be there when they were born. But if it wasn't for him they wouldn't have the chance to grow up somewhere like this. Hugo didn't do anything else for them, but he gave them this and I'm keeping it in trust for them.'

'Is that the only reason you don't want to sell?' asked Cal carefully. It was a fair enough reason, he supposed, but the security of an income ought to mean more to the boys in the future. He would be able to make her see the sense of that.

'No.' Cal could see the starlight gleaming in the huge dark eyes as Juliet turned to face him. 'I don't want to sell Wilparilla because I love it.'

She looked back at the darkness. 'It's funny, you know,' she said, almost to herself. 'When Hugo told me he'd bought a cattle station, I thought he was joking. One minute I was in London, the next I was *here*! It was awful at first. Everything was so strange. I hated the flies and the heat and the emptiness and the silence.'

'So what changed?'

He thought at first that Juliet wouldn't answer. 'Kit and Andrew changed it for me,' she said slowly at last. 'Hugo never wanted me to have a baby. He thought it would be too much of a tie, and my pregnancy disgusted him. We hadn't been married very long, and I was still clinging to the delusion that I could change him,' she added rather bitterly.

'Of course, Hugo didn't want to be changed. He used to spend most of his time in Sydney. He said he was sorting out details for the new homestead, but I don't suppose he was. Meanwhile I was here, hoping that everything would be magically different as soon as he saw his own children. I used to walk along the creek,' she remembered. 'And one day, I felt one of the babies move. I felt...'

Juliet trailed off, searching for the words to make Cal understand what had happened to her that day. 'I can't describe how I felt,' she admitted at last. 'But everything changed for me then. I think, in an odd way, I grew up then,' she said seriously. 'Wilparilla would be my babies' home, and I started to see it as they might see it. I started to listen to the birds and to smell the bush. I grew to love the light and the space and the silence and now...now I couldn't bear to leave it.'

Cal said nothing. He didn't want to know this. He wanted to go on thinking of her as an alien, an outsider, not as someone who felt about Wilparilla the way he did.

There was a long, long silence. Somewhere in the darkness, an insect whirred.

'We'd better get some sleep,' said Cal at last. He put his mug on the floor and stood up. He wished he could go to bed and wake up not knowing how much Juliet loved Wilparilla, not knowing how her husband had left her alone while she was pregnant. He wished he could be angry with her again. He wished he hadn't noticed how long and slender her legs were beneath the skimpy nightdress, or how the fine material moulded over her breasts.

Juliet nodded. The chair was deep and not easy to get out of without a concerted effort. She struggled to sit up, and without thinking Cal leant down to take her hand and pull her to her feet.

His fingers were warm and strong around hers, and Juliet was conscious of a ridiculous desire to cling to them. For the first time she became aware that he was bare-chested, and at the same moment realised how revealing her nightdress was. He was standing very close, still gripping her hand to steady her.

'OK?' he asked, and she nodded, intensely grateful for the darkness which hid the burning colour in her cheeks.

'Thank you,' she muttered.

There was an imperceptible hesitation, then Cal dropped her hand and stepped back. 'Don't think about it all any more tonight,' he said almost roughly. 'We'll sort something out in the morning.'

CHAPTER FOUR

THERE was no sign of Cal again when Juliet woke the next morning. He was probably avoiding her, Juliet thought in embarrassment, remembering how she had wept all over him the night before. She cringed when she thought of the helpless way she had just sat there and let him take control, of the wobbling hysteria in her voice and her self-pitying tears. He must think that she was pathetic!

But if Cal did think that, he gave no sign of it when he walked into the kitchen later that morning. Juliet had been baking, and there was a smudge of flour on her cheek. She flushed when she saw him, and her heart quickened, leaving her ridiculously breathless.

'I wanted to thank you for last night,' she said awkwardly. 'I was in a bit of a state, but I...well, I didn't mean to bore you with all my problems in the middle of the night. I'm sorry.'

'I'm glad you told me,' said Cal. He hesitated. He had been doing a lot of thinking that morning. 'I'm the one who should apologise,' he said. 'I didn't realise what you'd been through, and I think I was a bit unfair on you before.'

Juliet brushed flour slowly from her hands. 'That doesn't matter. I just wish all the problems you told me about yesterday would go away as easily.'

'They're not going to go away,' he told her frankly. 'We can make a start on some of them, though. I've sent two of the men out to fix the pipes at Okey Bore, and

the others are making a start on the fencing, but I think
you and I need to sit down and consider how we're
going to tackle the bigger problems. Are you up to that?'

'Now?'

'I think it would be best. You're going to have to
make some tough decisions, and the sooner the better.'

'All right.' Juliet untied her apron and draped it over
the back of the chair. She could hear the twins playing
outside on the verandah, where Natalie had volunteered
to keep an eye on them. She sat down at the kitchen
table and Cal spread out some papers before her.

'I've drawn up a list of jobs that need to be tackled
urgently,' he explained. 'Those on this sheet are essential, but not immediate, and then this third sheet shows
things that would improve the station in the long term.'

Juliet picked up the sheets of paper and eyed them in
dismay. The urgent list was even longer than the 'essential' one. 'We'll never be able to do all of that!'

'We can try,' said Cal bracingly. 'It depends how
much money you're prepared to put into saving
Wilparilla.'

She put down the last sheet. 'I haven't got any
money,' she said, and he frowned.

'You must have something. You don't buy properties
like these without a lot of capital behind you.'

'I know. There was plenty of money when we first
came out to Australia, but it's all gone.'

'*Gone?*' Cal stared at her. 'What on?'

Juliet lifted her shoulders wearily. 'Who knows? This
house cost a huge amount of money, but it was just one
of Hugo's whims. He would wake up in the morning
with an idea, and he wouldn't care how much it cost.
He always had a plan that was going to change every-

thing, but he never stuck at anything long enough to make it work.'

She smiled a little painfully, thinking that it was as true of her marriage as of anything else. 'Hugo could be very generous when he felt like it. He'd buy something incredibly expensive, just on a whim, and then give it away when he was tired of it. Everything came too easily to Hugo,' she added reflectively. 'He never had to fight for anything he wanted, so he didn't value what he had.

'You'd have to have met Hugo to understand what he was like,' she went on, seeing the disbelief in Cal's face. How could she explain her husband to a man like Cal? 'He could be cruel and irresponsible, but nobody could be more charming or better company when he felt like it. He had a sort of magnetism. And he was so handsome! He had a glamour too, with just the right undercurrent of dangerous unpredictability to make him irresistible. Even women who disapproved of everything he stood for fell for him.'

Once it had hurt just to say Hugo's name. Now she could talk about him dispassionately, as if he were a character in a book that she had read. 'Hugo was famous for never committing himself. He always had at least three beautiful women in tow: one he was finishing an affair with, one he was starting an affair with and one he had his eye on for the next affair.'

'Why would you want to get involved with someone like that?' The words were out before Cal could help himself, and Juliet half smiled. She should have known that Cal wouldn't understand about Hugo. She might as well have been describing an alien from Mars for all the two men had in common.

'Men with dangerous reputations are notoriously seductive,' she tried to explain, even though she knew that it was useless. 'Each of us secretly thought that all Hugo needed was the love of a good woman. Every woman who met him believed deep down that *she* would know how to handle him.'

'And out of all these women who wanted to save him, he chose you?'

'I know, it's hard to believe, isn't it?' said Juliet, accepting his surprise without rancour. 'I was just like everyone else, in love with him from afar at first. I was working in London then, and I saw him at a few parties, but mostly I knew about him from what I read in the gossip columns.'

'How did you meet him?' asked Cal, unwillingly drawn into her story.

'At a polo match. I was staying with friends for the weekend and he turned out to be friend of a friend of theirs. Close to, he was mesmerising. I was very young, only twenty-one, and Hugo swept me off my feet. I'd never met anyone like him before and I was lost. I didn't care about his reputation. I really thought he had changed for me.'

Juliet sighed, half-indulgent, half sad for that younger, naive self. 'When he asked me to marry him, I believed that proved it. Everyone told me not to marry him. My family and friends said that I was making the biggest mistake of my life, but I wouldn't listen. We had a big society wedding, and I wore a long white dress, and I was so sure that I would prove them all wrong.'

She shook her head at herself. Remembering those early days with Hugo still hurt more than she wanted to admit, and she got restlessly to her feet to make some coffee. Part of her wanted to tell Cal all this, to explain what Hugo had been like, but another part was afraid that he would think her a fool for being so stupid and gullible.

'Was it such a big mistake?' Cal asked reluctantly. He imagined Juliet as a bride, young and in love, and then he looked at her averted face as she filled the kettle, the shadowed eyes, the hurt that seemed to be carved into the contours of her cheeks, and he wondered what kind of man could do that to her. 'He wouldn't have married you if he hadn't loved you, would he?' he forced himself to say, although somehow the idea of Hugo loving her even briefly was jarring and unpleasant.

'Well, that's what I thought, of course.' Juliet spooned coffee from the jar into two mugs and kept her voice deliberately light. 'I thought, Hugo could have had anyone he wanted, but he chose me, so he must love me.'

'Why else would he marry you?'

She turned and leant against the unit while she waited for the kettle to boil, clasping her arms lightly together. She had gone so far; she might as well tell Cal it all.

'He married me because I was young and so pathetically grateful to him for choosing me that I wouldn't make trouble. I didn't know until after the wedding that his parents had made marriage a condition of settling his debts. When Hugo ran out of money, which he frequently did, he would just ask his parents to bail him out, but he was running up such enormous debts that they decided they needed to do something about it.

'I gather they thought a wife might be a stabilising influence on him,' Juliet continued, 'but of course I made absolutely no difference to Hugo's life at all. Once he was married they handed over the money, and he just carried on as before, spending wildly, having affairs, risking his neck on speedboats and skis, in fast cars and planes, whenever life got too tame for him. He was very easily bored,' she added ironically as the kettle boiled and she turned to fill the mugs.

'Why didn't you just leave him?' Cal asked, thinking that if he had ever met Hugo Laing in person he would have taken great pleasure in kicking him off his property.

Juliet carried the mugs over to the table. 'Because I was still young enough to think that it was all my fault for not being the right kind of wife for him, and I knew that if I did leave him, everyone would just say, "I told you it wouldn't work." At the time, it seemed less humiliating to try and salvage something from the marriage.

'Then Hugo ran into more trouble with his family. They were so wealthy that he didn't need to work, but the Laings are very keen on appearances, and for form's sake he had been given a job in their merchant bank. He didn't spend much time there, but when he did he had to make things more exciting by speculating wildly with their reserves.' She poured milk into her coffee and then held the jug up to Cal. 'Milk?'

He shook his head and she put the milk jug back in the fridge. 'I'm still not sure exactly what he was doing,' she confessed, 'but he was sailing even closer to the wind than usual, and his parents decided it would be better if Hugo was out of the country for a while. They've got huge business interests in Sydney, so we were packed off there—the unspoken message being that if I'd been a better wife, he would have settled down.'

'I didn't realise the English still thought of Australia as a useful place to send the black sheep of the family,' said Cal dryly.

'The Laings probably don't realise the British Empire no longer exists,' Juliet told him. 'If they weren't so arrogant and manipulative, they'd be laughable.'

Cal drank his coffee thoughtfully. 'It's still a long way from Sydney to Wilparilla,' he said. 'Don't tell me the Laings have got business interests in the outback as well?'

'No, buying Wilparilla was a classic Hugo whim. He liked Sydney for a while, and then he got bored. He went sailing one day with someone who had something to do with selling outback properties, and by the time he came home he'd put in an offer.'

Cal's mouth tightened when he thought how casually Wilparilla had changed hands. He knew exactly who Hugo had been sailing with.

'So here I am,' said Juliet. 'It was only when we got here that Hugo realised the advantages of an isolated property. He was furious when he found out I was pregnant, but that turned out to be a good excuse to leave me here once he got bored—which of course he did— so that he could fly off to Sydney or Perth or up to South East Asia on his own.'

'Why did you put up with it?' demanded Cal almost angrily.

Juliet ran her hands through her hair. It was hard to remember now. 'Because when we first came to Australia I hoped it would be a fresh start for us, and it was, at first. Hugo wasn't always a bastard. When he felt like it, he could be charming and funny and *exciting,* and I loved him. It takes a long time to give up loving someone like Hugo. It's like an addiction. You keep on hoping, even when you know it's no use.' She gave a tiny sigh. 'I *did* hope that once the twins were born Hugo would love them, and learn to love me because of them, but it didn't work out that way.'

'I'm sorry,' said Cal. It sounded inadequate, but what else was there to say?

'It was horrible,' Juliet acknowledged. 'I was desperately unhappy for a long time, but I'm not unhappy any more. Now I'm angry. I'm angry that Hugo made no effort to give his sons even one happy memory of him. I'm angry at the way he neglected Wilparilla, and most of all I'm angry that he made no financial provision for the boys. There was one insurance policy on his life, but most of that had to go on settling his outstanding debts, and what's left has to keep the boys and I until Wilparilla is making a profit again.'

'You realise that could be some time, unless you can inject a large amount of cash now?' Cal asked as gently as he could.

Juliet bit her lip. 'How long?'

This was his chance, Cal realised. He could tell her ten, fifteen years, and she would give up. She wouldn't risk what little money the boys had. Wilparilla would be his for the asking.

'What about your husband's parents?' he heard his voice asking instead. 'Couldn't you approach them for some money? Kit and Andrew are their grandchildren, after all.'

'No.' Juliet's mouth hardened. 'I don't want anything to do with them. I don't trust them. They don't think they have to play by the same rules as anyone else. If I took money from them, they'd think they had the right to interfere in my life. They'd be out here, lording it over everybody, looking for profit, wanting to take the twins back to England...no, I won't ask them for anything.'

'What about the banks?'

What was he *doing*? Cal asked himself desperately. He was supposed to be encouraging Juliet to sell, not suggesting ways she could save Wilparilla for herself.

But Juliet was shaking her head. 'I've got a huge over-draft as it is, and they won't lend me money on the kind of terms I need.'

'All right, so we'll just have to do what we can with-out investment.' Cal shut his mind to the warning voice telling him that he was on the verge of blowing his best chance to get Wilparilla back, and picked up the list of urgent jobs. He studied it, frowning slightly.

'We've got four men out there, and it won't do them any harm to do some work for a change,' he said. 'We'll have to do without any contractors. That means no heli-copters for the musters, no bull-catchers. We'll have to do all that ourselves.'

He rubbed his chin thoughtfully, and Juliet found her-self noticing the golden hairs on his forearm, the solidity of his thigh on the chair next to hers. He was wearing shorts, and the impulse to lay her hand against his skin tingled in her palm. She looked away hastily.

'Repairs are a major problem, especially for the ve-hicles,' he went on, oblivious to Juliet's distraction. 'If we can't invest in new machinery, we'll just have to salvage what we've got, and to do that we need a decent mechanic. These guys wouldn't know a spanner if it jumped up and smacked them between the eyes. I know just the man we need,' he went on with a glance at Juliet, who cleared her throat and tried to look as if she had been concentrating all along. 'We'd have to pay him, but it will be worth it.'

Dropping the list back onto the table, Cal stood up. 'I'll go and ring him now,' he said, and then stopped, remembering a little too late that he wasn't the one pay-ing the wages. 'If that's OK with you, of course?'

Juliet smiled weakly. 'Of course,' she said.

In a way it was a relief to have him out of the room.

Juliet lifted her hands and saw to her horror that they were shaking slightly. One minute Cal had been an advisor, an experienced manager, and the next she had looked at him and seen a man—a man with a tanned, tough body, a man with steady eyes and a mouth that made her feel weak just looking at it.

The memory of how that mouth had felt against hers uncurled dangerously in the pit of her stomach.

She mustn't think about it, Juliet told herself desperately. That kiss was better forgotten. She and Cal had obviously got off on the wrong foot, that was all. It was hard to believe now how cold and hostile she had found him, how angry he had made her feel that first day. Only yesterday she had thought that she hated him, and now...

Now he was just doing the job she was paying him to do, Juliet told herself firmly. She didn't have to feel anything about him. Cal was her manager, and that was all.

'We're in luck.' In spite of herself, Juliet's heart leapt as Cal came back from the office. 'I rang Sam, and he's had enough of retirement. He can get here by next week.'

'Good.' It came out as no more than a squeak, and Cal looked at Juliet curiously. She cleared her throat. 'Great,' she tried again.

'I've arranged a housekeeper, too,' he added casually, and her jaw dropped.

'A *housekeeper*?'

'We're going to need all the hands we can get,' said Cal. 'You'll be more useful if you're not tied by the children and the cooking.'

'I'd love to be useful,' said Juliet, 'but I'm not sure I will be. I don't know how to do anything useful,' she admitted, shame-faced.

'You can learn,' said Cal. 'In any case, you can probably do more than you think. There's a lot of time-consuming paperwork in the office, and if nothing else you can check fences and water troughs. I presume you can drive?'

She nodded. 'Well, then,' he said, 'there's no reason why you shouldn't learn to ride as well—we'll need all the horsemen we can get on the musters if we can't afford any helicopters—but you can't do any of that until you've got someone to look after the house and the kids while you're out.'

Juliet had opened her mouth to tell him that she already knew how to ride perfectly well, but his last words diverted her. 'I can see that,' she admitted worriedly, 'but I can't afford a housekeeper, especially not if I'm paying for a mechanic.'

'You don't need to worry about that,' said Cal gruffly. 'I'll sort that out.'

She stared at him. 'Why should you do that?'

'I was going to get a housekeeper myself for Natalie,' he pointed out, not quite meeting her eye. 'Someone has to keep an eye on her while she does her schoolwork.'

He wondered how he had got himself into the position of not only helping Juliet stay at Wilparilla but paying for it out of his own pocket. It would work out to his advantage in the end, Cal reassured himself. If he helped Juliet now, she would come to rely on him, and would trust him all the more later on when he told her that her only option was to sell.

'I've been talking to my aunt,' he went on, before he could question his motives too closely. 'Maggie grew up in the outback but she left when she got married and her husband got a job in Melbourne. She's widowed now, and she wants to come back. She knew I wanted to come back, too, and she suggested some time ago that she should come and look after Natalie for me if the job worked out.'

'I can't ask her to look after two boys under three as well as Natalie,' Juliet protested.

'Maggie doesn't mind. She's always said that she's only interested in people under six or over sixty, so the boys will suit her fine. She can be a bit scary as far as the rest of us are concerned, but for some reason kids love her. They'd be completely safe with Maggie.'

'She sounds wonderful,' said Juliet, weakening. The thought of being able to hand over the cooking and leave the boys without worrying every second they were out of sight was almost too good to be true.

'There is just one condition,' said Cal. 'Maggie says she's too old and crotchety to share a house any more. She's happy to spend the day here, but she wants a house of her own to go back to in the evenings.' He hesitated slightly. 'I said we'd fix up the manager's house and she could have that.'

'That would mean you and Natalie would stay on at the homestead?'

'Yes.'

'Won't you mind that?' Juliet asked rather self-consciously.

'Not if you don't.'

Cal's voice was very even. Juliet stole a glance at him and then found that she couldn't look away. His eyes were a keen, cool grey and they held her suspended, unable to move, while her heart began a slow, slamming beat that reverberated through her and stopped the breath in her throat.

She moistened her lips. 'No, I don't mind,' she croaked.

'That's settled, then.' Cal had to remind himself to breathe. She really did have extraordinary eyes, so deep and blue that you could easily get lost in them, eyes that made you disturbingly aware of the softness of her lips and the scent of her skin.

There was a silence. It seemed to loop around them as they stood there and looked at each other, shortening the air and prickling over their skin. It should have been easy to break it, to move on or to leave, but somehow it wasn't.

'Dad! Juliet! Come and see this!' Natalie's peal of laughter from the verandah shattered the tension and they both jumped.

Intensely grateful for the diversion, Cal followed Juliet outside. It was immediately obvious what had caused Natalie's amusement. Kit and Andrew had found a couple of plastic buckets and were showing off, putting them over their heads and staggering around to make Natalie laugh. By the time Juliet and Cal came through the screen door they were getting cocky, and in the middle of clowning around with the buckets on their heads they managed to bump into each other with such an impact that they both sailed backwards to land with a thump on their bottoms.

They looked so ridiculous that Cal and Juliet couldn't help laughing. Belatedly realising that their audience had increased, Kit and Andrew lifted their buckets at exactly the same time and peeked out from beneath them. They were so obviously delighted with the reaction that Cal grinned and glanced at Juliet.

The sight of her laughing stopped him dead. He had never seen her smile like that before, he realised with something of a shock. It transformed her, lighting the dark eyes with love, banishing the shadows, dazzling him with its warmth and beauty.

As if sensing his stare, Juliet turned her head, still laughing, only to find her gaze locked with his once more. Something in his expression made her catch her breath, and her smile faltered. 'What is it?' she asked uncertainly.

'Nothing.' Cal's eyes shuttered. 'I'd better go and see how the men are getting on,' he said, pulling himself together with an effort. 'We'll work out a plan of action tonight.'

'OK.' Juliet watched him turn towards the steps. 'Cal?' she said on an impulse.

He looked over his shoulder, lifting an interrogative eyebrow.

'Thank you,' she said simply. It wasn't much to express what it meant to her to know that he had taken charge, to know that from now on things were going to change, but she hoped that he would understand what she was trying to say.

Cal didn't answer directly. Instead he came back to her. 'You've got flour on your cheek,' was all he said. Very gently, he wiped it off with his thumb, barely grazing her skin, and then he turned once more, and was down the steps and into the harsh outback glare.

Juliet stood there, her gaze unfocused and one hand to her cheek where he had touched her, looking out at the sunlight long after he had disappeared.

They agreed that night that their first priority was to do up the manager's house so that Maggie could take over the housework.

Juliet was keeping herself under close control. She had been shaken by the way Cal had made her feel that morning, by the desire that had jolted through her at the mere thought of touching him, but more by the feeling that he had shouldered the burden that had been weighing her down for so long. The relief was acute, but it also left her feeling vaguely uneasy. She had forgotten what it was like to share her worries. Marriage to Hugo had taught her that the only person she could rely on was herself. It would be a mistake to start leaning on anyone else.

It was just that Cal would be a very easy man to lean on, if she let herself.

'If you can get someone to do the repairs, I can clean the house and give it all a coat of paint,' she told Cal, keeping her voice deliberately cool and businesslike. 'At least I can do that with the children.'

Cal was glad to follow her lead and keep the discussion impersonal. He couldn't satisfactorily explain to himself why he had acted as he had to help Juliet sort out the mess that was Wilparilla. All he knew was that something had changed last night, and when he had looked into her eyes this morning it had changed again. He wanted to go back to hating her, but he couldn't, and now he didn't know what he felt about her.

He didn't have to feel anything about her, Cal told himself. In fact, it would be better if he didn't. Much easier to do as Juliet was doing and pretend that the air had never tightened between them that morning, that he had never stood looking foolishly into her eyes and remembering how it had felt to kiss her.

Juliet worked all week on the house. Every morning the boys rode their tricycles round and round in the yard while Natalie did her lessons sitting at the radio. Juliet had to throw out boxes and boxes of rubbish before she could even start cleaning, but there was something therapeutic about clearing everything out and then setting to with a scrubbing brush. For Juliet, restoring the house to a pristine state became a challenge, her way of proving to Cal that she could work as hard as he could.

He found her there one afternoon, on her knees in one of the bedrooms. She was wearing a grubby T-shirt and faded shorts, and her face was scarlet from heat and effort. When he called her name from the hall, she sat back on her heels and wiped her face with the back of her forearm, leaving smears of damp dust and dirt.

Cal stopped in the doorway. Unbidden came the memory of Juliet that first fateful night, cool and elegant in her turquoise dress. The Juliet he saw now might be a different woman, with her dirty face and damp hair clinging to her neck, and her hands wrinkled from a week of dipping a scrubbing brush in water.

She was certainly a woman he liked much better.

In spite of an aching back every night, Juliet was happier than she had been for a long, long time. The shadowed look had gone from her eyes, and the brittle tension was slowly seeping from her muscles. No longer did her shoulders feel rigid as boards when she woke every morning.

In the evenings, after the children had gone to bed, they would share a beer on the verandah and talk about plans for the next day. Over supper, they worked out an action plan for the next few months. The mechanic had arrived and was already getting the machinery back in working order—or so Juliet heard. Sam was so shy that he had just muttered a greeting and stumped off, and she hadn't seen him since, but Cal seemed to think that was quite normal. He explained what Sam was doing, and told her about the yearly routine on the station and Juliet learnt to make sense of the accounts, but that was all they talked about, and when the meal was over they would say goodnight politely and separate in the corridor.

By tacit agreement, they kept the conversation strictly impersonal. Juliet was very aware of Cal as he sat across the table from her, and she would watch his face as he talked. She grew to know his gestures, the way he narrowed his eyes when considering a difficult question, the way he rubbed his chin as he thought, the deft movements of his hands.

Part of her longed to know him better. She wanted to ask him about growing up in the outback, she wanted him to tell her about his wife and what he had really felt about all those housekeepers Natalie had said used to fall in love with him. But Cal never offered any information about himself, and she was chary about letting herself get too close.

Juliet didn't want to spoil what she had. It was such bliss to have someone to talk to at last, to feel that she had a real role to play at Wilparilla after all. If she thought too much about the lean length of his body, or the crease in his cheek when he smiled, she knew that the carefully impersonal atmosphere they had created would crumble.

It was hard enough to preserve it as it was. Every night Cal helped her wash up after supper, and every night they studiously avoided thinking about the kiss they had shared. It was never mentioned between them, but for Juliet it still shimmered dangerously in the air between them, ready to leap into life at the slightest brush of Cal's arm against hers.

Each time he laid the tea-towel down her heart would leap, remembering how he had crossed over to her and calmly pulled her arms aside so that he could put his

hands at her waist. Each time she wondered if he would
do the same thing again, but he never did, and Juliet
would say goodnight and go to bed alone, hating herself
for being disappointed.

CHAPTER FIVE

IT WAS much easier when they could spend their days working, but by the time the next weekend came round Juliet realised guiltily that Cal hadn't yet had any time off. 'Tomorrow's Sunday,' she reminded him on the Saturday evening. 'I think we could all do with a day off.'

'I was planning to catch some of those old scrubber bulls,' Cal protested, but Juliet overrode him.

'The bulls can wait,' she said. 'And that's an order!' She passed him the dish of roast pumpkin to forestall any further argument. 'Natalie needs to spend some time alone with you,' she reminded him, and the angry look that had sprung into Cal's eyes at the reminder of his subservient position faded.

'You're right,' he said slowly. 'Thanks...boss.'

He had been so busy recently that he was guiltily aware that he hadn't been spending as much time with his daughter as he would normally do. On some days he had only finished in time to kiss her goodnight.

Not that Natalie seemed to mind. She was always full of chatter about what Kit and Andrew had been doing, or how Juliet had allowed her to help with the cleaning. She had blossomed since he had brought her back to Wilparilla, and however much Cal tried to tell himself that it was being away from the city that had made the difference, he knew deep down that much of Natalie's happiness was due to Juliet and the twins.

Natalie was thrilled at breakfast the next morning

when Cal asked her if she would like to go riding. 'There's a pony in the paddock that should be just about right for you,' he told her as she threw her arms around his neck in excitement.

As she danced off to put on her oldest jeans, Cal looked across the table at Juliet. 'I hope you're going to have a day off as well,' he said with a touch of awkwardness. It wasn't up to him to tell her what to do, but he wouldn't enjoy his day much knowing that she was in the office slaving over paperwork or down at the house painting. She looked as if she needed to relax more than he did.

'I shall sit on the verandah with a book, if Kit and Andrew let me read any of it,' Juliet told him, determinedly bright.

The prospect of a quiet day alone with her small sons should have been a tempting one, but somehow Juliet couldn't help feeling rather forlorn as she stood on the verandah with her book and saw Cal walk off towards the paddock with that easy, deliberate stride of his, his daughter skipping happily along beside him, their hats sitting at exactly the same angle. In spite of the difference in their height, they looked absolutely right together.

As Juliet watched, Natalie tucked her hand confidingly into Cal's and he turned his head to smile down at her. She had worried that Cal wasn't spending enough time with his daughter, but the bond between them was such an obviously loving one that Juliet felt absurd tears prick her eyes.

The homestead felt very empty when they had gone. Kit, who had wanted to go with Natalie and Cal, was cross, and Andrew soon picked up on his fretful mood.

Juliet sighed, and was just abandoning her attempt to open the book when Andrew cried out in delight.

'Horses!'

Riding towards them were Natalie and Cal, leading a solid-looking bay mare behind them. They stopped at the bottom of the verandah steps. 'Natalie's been telling me the boys have never been on a horse,' said Cal.

Juliet stood at the top of the steps, holding Kit and Andrew by the hand. Her chest felt tight, but she was smiling giddily at the realisation that they had not been forgotten after all. 'No,' she managed to say. 'I've never been able to hold two of them on at the same time.'

Cal wished she wouldn't smile like that. It wasn't good for his breathing. 'If you think you can manage to hold one up before you, I'll take the other, and they can have their first ride. Would you like that, boys?'

'Yes! Yes! Ride!' they shouted as he dismounted easily, and Juliet let go of their small hands so that they could run down the steps and jump up and down beside him, clamouring to be allowed on first.

Cal was laughing as he tried to quell their excitement, and Juliet, watching him with her sons, felt something twist painfully inside her. If only Kit and Andrew could have had a father like Cal. 'I'll get their hats,' she muttered, and went inside before Cal could notice the tears stinging her eyes.

'Have you been on a horse before?' he asked when she reappeared and had jammed a hat on each of the boys.

'Once or twice,' said Juliet, who had at one time thought seriously about a professional show-jumping career.

Cal missed the dryness in her voice. He took hold of the bay's bridle and led it forward. 'We'll take it very easy,' he reassured her. 'She's a lazy old girl, so she won't do anything alarming.'

'Good,' said Juliet, thinking it would be sensible to start the boys off on a quiet horse. She would reserve the pleasure of showing Cal how well she could ride for a later occasion.

Keeping hold of the horse's bridle with one hand, Cal moved to give her a leg up, but, to his approval, she had already mounted and was sitting demurely in the saddle. 'OK, who's going with Mum?' he asked, and without waiting for an answer scooped up Andrew, who squealed with excitement at finding himself so high.

'Me! Me!' shouted Kit, as Juliet settled Andrew in the saddle in front of her.

'Come on then, you,' said Cal, throwing him up onto his horse and mounting himself in one fluid movement.

Completely at home on her pony, Natalie circled round them as they rode slowly along the creek. Overhead, the birds wheeled and screeched in the trees and the horses blew softly through their noses, shaking their manes against the flies. Kit and Andrew were entranced. Juliet could feel the rigid excitement in Andrew's body settled securely against hers, and when she looked across at Kit his eyes were like saucers and his smile was wide with delight.

'Does Andrew look that happy?' she asked, catching Cal's eye, and he nodded and smiled.

'As a pig in pooh.'

Juliet laughed. Their gazes held a fraction longer than necessary, and then both looked away. Cal kept his eyes on the horizon and reminded himself of all the reasons he should never think about kissing her again. Juliet concentrated on watching the birds while Cal's smile shimmered still before her eyes. Even without looking at him, she could picture him with absolute clarity, his face shadowed by his hat, the line of his jaw, the easy way he sat on the horse, one hand resting on his thigh, the other holding the reins while Kit nestled into the hard security of his body.

Lucky Kit, thought Juliet, before she could help herself.

They stopped by a shallow pool shaded by a gnarled, leaning gum. The horses waited patiently, tails flicking, as Natalie and the boys took off their jeans and splashed happily together in the dappled water. Juliet and Cal sat carefully apart on a rock and kept their eyes on the children so they couldn't look at each other.

The water was limpid with silence, and on the far side of the creek the trees admired their unwavering reflection beneath a deep blue sky. 'It's beautiful,' sighed Juliet after a while.

'Haven't you been here before?'

'No.' She shook her head rather sadly. 'You've only been here a couple of weeks and already you know Wilparilla better than I do.'

Cal didn't answer immediately. The knowledge of how greatly he was deceiving Juliet was making him increasingly uncomfortable, but he wasn't prepared to give up his dream of buying Wilparilla back yet. Natalie's happiness was at stake as much as his own. Even her initial disappointment at finding that the homestead had changed completely and that she couldn't remember any of it had disappeared, and she loved it all.

'I wanted to thank you for what you've done for Natalie,' he said, deliberately changing the subject.

Surprised, Juliet glanced at him, only to find that he had risked a glance at her at the same time. She jerked her gaze sternly back to the children. 'I haven't done anything for Natalie,' she said. 'It's the other way round, if anything. She's such a happy, helpful little girl.'

'She is now,' said Cal, watching his daughter shrieking in the water. 'It's not that long since I had a battle to get her to school every morning. She wouldn't talk to anyone or do anything.'

'Really?' Juliet's eyes rested on Natalie as well. 'It seems hard to believe, looking at her now. What was the matter?'

'She was unhappy,' he said simply. 'I kept asking her if anything was wrong and she'd say no, and then one day I caught her in tears and everything came out.' He stopped, remembering how guilty he had felt for not realising sooner how miserable his daughter had been.

'It was my fault,' he went on slowly. 'I should have realised how much she hated her school. She never fitted in, and children can be cruel sometimes to outsiders.'

'Was she being bullied?' asked Juliet in concern.

'Oh, I don't think it was as bad as that. She just never felt as if she belonged. I think she was homesick.' Cal grimaced. 'She was only five when we moved to Brisbane, but her whole life had been spent in the outback, and she didn't adapt as I'd hoped she would. I didn't adapt that well either,' he admitted. 'I missed the bush, but I pretended I didn't to make it easier for Natalie. I could see that she wasn't happy, but if I asked her what was wrong, she would always say everything was OK.'

Juliet risked another glance at him. 'If Natalie was happy in the outback, why did you move?'

She thought for a moment that Cal wouldn't answer, but he did. 'Because it was what Sara would have wanted,' he said. 'I'd grown up on a station, but Sara was from Brisbane. She was the sister of one of my schoolfriends. I met her when she was sixteen, so we'd known each other for five years before we were married, and she'd been to visit plenty of times, but it was still hard for her when we were first married. Being a visitor is fine, but it's different when you suddenly find yourself left alone all day, hundreds of miles from the nearest shop when you're used to living in a city.'

Cal glanced at Juliet. 'You'd understand what it was like for her,' he said. 'Sara was lonely.'

'Yes, I do understand,' said Juliet, but it hadn't been the same. Hugo had been absent so often that she had been left literally on her own. She hadn't been Cal's bride, and he hadn't come home to her at the end of each day, glad to see her, ready to take her in his arms and make all the loneliness worthwhile. Juliet didn't think she would have found it hard to adapt to the outback life if she had been married to Cal instead of Hugo.

'She really tried,' Cal went on, ignorant of Juliet's mental interruption, 'but she never felt at home here, and after Natalie was born, she started talking about wanting her to have a normal life. She didn't think it was healthy for a child to grow up so isolated, and I think in a way she was right. Natalie was perfectly happy, but she didn't know what it was like to play with other children—and that made it much more difficult for her when she did get to a city. If she'd had brothers or sisters, it might have been different, but she never got the chance to find out.'

'What happened?' asked Juliet softly.

'Sara died giving birth to a baby boy.' Cal's voice was utterly emotionless. 'She used to worry about being so far from a hospital, but all those doctors and all that technology didn't help her when it mattered. She had eclampsia.'

Juliet put a hand to her mouth in distress. 'Oh, no.'

Cal looked across the creek. 'They took her into hospital as soon as they spotted the signs, but she started fitting and they couldn't stop it.' His jaw tightened. 'Cardiac arrest, they told me. They said there was nothing they could do.'

'And the baby?'

He shook his head. 'They did an emergency Caesarean, but it was too late. He died a few hours later. He was called Ben. That was what Sara had wanted.'

The short, staccato sentences moved Juliet more than any eloquent expression of grief would have done. She could see his suffering in the rigid line of his mouth, hear it in the tight control of his voice, and she was ashamed of her own self-pitying display that night on the verandah. What had she had to endure compared to Cal, who had lost his wife and his son on the same day?

Without thinking, she reached out and touched his hand. 'I'm so sorry,' she said quietly, and Cal, turning his head at her touch, saw that there were tears in her eyes. Somehow he found his fingers curled tightly around hers.

'It's all right,' he said, as if she was the one needing comfort. 'It's six years ago now. You get...' he hesitated, searching for the right word '... used to it, I guess. And I had Natalie. I just had to keep going.'

'How did you manage?' Juliet asked. 'She couldn't have been much older than the twins are now.'

'She was three.' Cal seemed to have forgotten that he was still holding her hand. 'My mother and sister helped out, but I had to get a housekeeper in the end. The trouble is, good housekeepers aren't easy to come by, and if they do the job well they don't stay long.'

'Natalie told me they all fell in love with you,' said Juliet dryly.

'Did she?' He laughed, but without much humour. 'We did have one or two embarrassing episodes, yes. They managed to fall in love without any encouragement from me. They were just bored, and falling in love must have seemed more fun than keeping the house clean and looking after Natalie.'

'Falling in love with someone who doesn't love you isn't usually much fun,' she pointed out, conscious of a faint pang of sympathy for those unknown girls who had tried to get through Cal's cool reserve, and very aware of his fingers, strong and firm around hers. Of course, *she* wouldn't do anything stupid like that—she had already learnt her lesson—but she could see how easily they must have fallen for him, especially if he had smiled the way he did sometimes...

'It certainly wasn't fun for me,' said Cal, bringing her back to the present. 'Once they realised I wasn't interested, they'd decide the situation was too awkward for them to stay and I'd have to find someone new. I could have lived with the disruption, but I was worried about Natalie. She'd just get to know one girl when another would appear.'

Juliet tried not to notice the cuffs of Cal's dark blue shirt were rolled back from his wrist and their forearms were *almost* touching. His closeness was making her feel giddy.

'It must have been very unsettling for her,' she managed, hoping Cal wouldn't notice the unsteadiness in her voice.

He didn't seem to. His eyes were on Natalie, his thoughts on that terrible time. 'In the end I didn't even bother with trying to find another housekeeper, and

Natalie came along and did whatever I was doing, but I knew I couldn't carry on like that for ever. Eventually she was going to need a woman around. I knew what Sara would have said. She'd wanted Natalie to go to a proper school and grow up knowing her cousins and family in Brisbane, just like she had done.'

Belatedly, Cal realised that he was still holding Juliet's hand, and faint colour tinged his cheekbones. He released her hurriedly with a murmur of embarrassed apology.

Juliet felt ridiculously self-conscious. Her palm burned where it had been pressed against his, and she didn't know what to do with her hand now that she had it back. She laid it on the smooth bark of the log they were sitting on, rested it on her knee, then tried tucking it under her other arm, but still it twitched and throbbed uncomfortably, as if the only place that would satisfy it was curled back between Cal's long, strong fingers.

There was a tiny, constrained silence. Juliet broke it after a moment. 'So you sold your station so that you could take Natalie to Brisbane?' Her voice sounded a little stilted, she thought, but she hoped that Cal wouldn't notice.

He sighed. 'Looking back, I wish I'd done things differently, but at the time selling the station seemed to be the only option. It was one of the hardest decisions I've ever had to make, but then it seemed that the only way to give Natalie some security and bring her up the way her mother would have wanted was to sell up and start a new life for both of us in the city.

'I did try,' he went on, as if Juliet had accused him of not making enough effort. 'I set up my own company so that I could work from the house and fit in with Natalie's school hours, and I made sure we did all those things you just can't do in the outback, like going out for a pizza or a movie, and we'd tell each other how good it was to be able to do those things.

'And then one day I found Natalie crying.' Cal's mouth twisted. 'She's a brave little kid,' he said. 'She hardly ever cries. But all the time I was pretending, to make things easier for her, *she* was pretending to make things easier for *me*. When I got it all out of her, she told me that all she wanted was to go home.'

'To live in the outback?'

'Yes.' He would have to be careful, Cal realised, rather late in the day. Juliet was a good listener. He never talked about Sara's death, or about his son who had only lived a few hours, but somehow he had found himself telling Juliet, and it had been oddly comforting. It would be all too easy to end up telling her the whole story, and he didn't want to think what would happen if she found out that Wilparilla had been their home, and that Natalie's distress had been all that it had taken to decide him on this pretence.

He hadn't thought about Juliet, or what she might feel. Friends on neighbouring properties had told him what had happened to Wilparilla since he had left, and to Cal, Juliet had just been a spoilt Englishwoman who was responsible for ruining his property and was making it impossible for him to make his daughter happy again by taking her home.

'That's when I heard that you were looking for a manager,' he said, picking his words with care. 'I didn't mind being a manager as long as Natalie was happy—and she is, now. That's all that matters at the moment. She'll have to go away to school at some stage, of course, but she's happy doing her lessons with the

School of the Air, and for now it's enough for us both just to be here.'

It was the first time he had told her anything significant about himself and what had brought him here. Juliet wondered how it was possible to feel that someone was so familiar when you knew so little about them.

'I didn't realise that you used to own a station of your own,' she said, trying to remember just what he *had* told her. 'I suppose I just assumed that you'd been a manager before,' she acknowledged, and then hesitated. Something in Cal's expression told her that he didn't want to talk about it, but she couldn't resist the temptation to find out more about him. 'Was it a property near here?'

'Yes,' said Cal curtly. He wanted to discourage her from asking any more questions so that he wouldn't have to lie to her.

Juliet wondered if he felt about it the way she felt about Wilparilla. 'Do you mind very much knowing that someone else owns it now?'

'Yes,' he said, and then, as if the thought had just occurred to him, 'Sometimes.' Cal looked at Juliet, almost puzzled. When had his obsession to regain Wilparilla as soon as possible faded into a mere aim, something important but not immediately essential? 'Not always,' he said slowly.

There was a tiny silence while Juliet readjusted her ideas. 'I would have thought you would hate being a manager if you've had your own station,' she said slowly. 'Why didn't you buy a property of your own?'

This was dangerous ground. Cal hunched his shoulders. 'Cattle stations don't come on the market that often,' he said, as casually as he could.

'But you're looking?'

'For the right place,' he said.

'I...I suppose if you find it, you'll want to leave?' Juliet made herself ask, horrified to find how desolate the thought of Wilparilla without Cal seemed already. She mustn't let herself rely on him too much.

'Yes,' said Cal, although it wasn't him who would be leaving. It would be Juliet. The thought was curiously disturbing. 'There's no immediate prospect of that, anyway,' he told her. 'I know what I want, and there's no sign that it's likely to be up for sale for a while yet. You needn't worry,' he added, reading the relief in her face, 'I won't leave before my trial period is up!'

Juliet had forgotten all about the trial. It seemed a very long time since she had insisted that Cal acknowledge her as boss. She had come to think of him as more of a partner, and now his words were like a splash of cold water, reminding her of the reality of the situation. Cal was her employee, not her partner. He hadn't forgotten it and neither should she.

'I'm glad to hear it,' she said, withdrawing imperceptibly. 'Of course, I hope for your sake you manage to find what you want,' she made herself go on, as if all she cared about was the potential inconvenience of having to find a new manager. 'I can see that it wouldn't be easy. As soon as Hugo died, the vultures were circling, putting in offers to buy Wilparilla.' A faint, angry flush stained her cheeks at the memory. 'He was killed in a car accident in Sydney, and I'd hardly got back from there when my lawyer was on the phone saying that someone had put in an offer for when I wanted to sell— and I've had others since.'

Cal winced inwardly. 'Were you never tempted to take any?'

'No, I wasn't!' snapped Juliet, eyes bright with remembered rage. 'I know what they thought! They thought I was just a pathetic little woman who'd never stick it out here on my own. They expected me to take the money and run, and no doubt when I didn't they thought I was just holding out for more!'

He *had* thought that. Cal remembered his fury each time his lawyer had rung him to tell him that his increased offer had been dismissed in no uncertain terms.

'I wasn't going to be bullied off my own property!' Juliet went on, still ruffled at the thought of the offers.

'Obviously whoever it was had never met you,' he said dryly. 'Otherwise they'd have known not to bother.'

'Yes, well.' Juliet's angry flush was fading. 'If anyone ever asks you if I'm interested in selling Wilparilla, you can tell them I've got no intention of going anywhere!'

'I will,' said Cal, but fortunately Juliet had looked away at a shout from one of the boys and missed the irony in his expression.

'Dad! Look at this rock!' Natalie galloped up to display what she had found in the shallow water at the edge of the creek. Kit and Andrew, anxious to share in the glory, crowded round Cal as well.

Juliet watched the way Andrew leant trustfully against him, the way Kit danced up and down to get his attention. Her eyes followed his gaze to Cal's face. He was dutifully admiring their find, and as she saw him smile she was shaken by a jolt of desire so pure and naked that she flinched.

She wanted the children to go away, so that she could slide along the log and lay her hand on his thigh as naturally as Andrew was doing. She wanted to lean into him and kiss his throat. She wanted to feel him turn and smile, to know that he would kiss her back, and that later, when all the children were in bed, he would take off her clothes and lay her down in the moonlight and make love to her until she wept.

Juliet leapt to her feet before her imagination could spin any further out of control. 'I think we'd better go back now,' she said, in a voice that was horribly high and cracked.

She was silent on the ride back to the homestead. Her earlier contentment had evaporated, leaving her edgy and unsure of what she really felt any more. Juliet didn't want to be hurt again as Hugo had hurt her. She had survived by detaching herself from the pain, by shutting part of herself off, and she was afraid that if she let anyone too close, they would shatter the seal that kept her strong.

When Juliet thought of her hand in Cal's, she knew how easy it would be to let her defences down, and she shied away instinctively from the idea. It was just as well he had reminded her of the real situation. She was paying him to be there, but he wouldn't always be. He had money of his own, and as soon as he found the right property he would be gone and she would be left alone again. There was no point in letting herself like him and there was certainly no point in desiring him. She was his employer and he was her employee, and it would be easier all round if it just stayed that way.

Cal sensed Juliet's withdrawal, and told himself he was glad. He regretted having told her as much as he had. She had made it plain enough that she wasn't going to sell Wilparilla, and what was the point of staying here if there was no chance of being able to buy it back?

If he had any sense, he would give up the whole idea of staying here as manager. The longer he stayed, the harder it would be to remember that wanting Wilparilla back meant wanting Juliet to leave. It had seemed a sensible idea at the time, but when Cal looked at Natalie's bright face as she rode beside him, chattering to the boys, he had a nasty feeling that somewhere along the line he had made a big mistake. As things were at the moment, Natalie would be heartbroken at the idea of them leaving Wilparilla again, and if Juliet wouldn't sell, he could find himself staying here for ever as a mere manager.

Cal scowled at the thought. He should have just persisted with the offers that Juliet had objected to so much. She would have accepted one in the end, and it would have been much better than getting to know her, learning how she turned her head and smiled, the gallant way she tilted her chin. It made Cal feel as if he was being dragged towards a precipice. If he let himself be pulled over the edge, he would find himself involved, and that was the last thing he wanted right now.

Mentally digging in his heels, Cal glanced sideways at Juliet, who was riding silently on the other side of Natalie, and he noticed for the first time how at home she looked in the saddle. For some reason this just made him feel even more disgruntled. Remembering to dislike her would be so much easier if she would just be the spoilt, selfish, supercilious woman he had first taken her to be. Juliet's failure to live down to his expectations left Cal feeling obscurely and unfairly resentful.

Juliet sensed his withdrawal too, and tried not to feel hurt. She should be grateful to him, she knew. They should have stuck to impersonal subjects, as they had done before. It would have been much better not to know about his wife and baby son, about his worries for his daughter, not to understand that he was a man with his own doubts and regrets, and not a superhuman manager who had given her real hope for Wilparilla for the first time in years.

If they had carried on as they were, she might not have noticed the line of his jaw or the creases round his eyes when he smiled. She wouldn't have known about the tingly strength of his fingers, and she wouldn't have thought about what it would be like if he wasn't her manager, if she could bring her horse up next to him and reach out to touch him—

But he *was* her manager, Juliet reminded herself sternly. So she couldn't—*wouldn't*—think about it any more.

CHAPTER SIX

IT WAS all very well deciding to keep things cool and impersonal, but not that easy in practice, Juliet realised early that evening. They were all in the kitchen, having supper together, and the twins, thoroughly over-excited after their ride, were showing off. Having discovered they could make Natalie giggle by pulling funny faces, they were egging each other on to ever greater facial contortions.

'That's enough,' said Juliet firmly. 'Stop being silly and eat your supper, or there'll be no birthday presents!'

Natalie was instantly alert at the prospect of a birthday. 'When is it?'

'Three weeks today,' said Juliet after a moment's calculation.

'Will they have a party, with a cake and candles and everything?'

'If they're good,' she said, with what was supposed to be a quelling look at the twins, who were too young to have grasped the concept of birthdays, or indeed of bribery in return for future good behaviour, and who were still playing up to their audience. 'Don't encourage them!' Juliet protested as Cal and Natalie continued to laugh, but it was impossible to keep her stern expression convincingly in place, and in the end she gave in and laughed too.

They looked like a family, she realised with a sudden pang. A happy family. But of course they weren't. If they were a family, she would be Cal's wife instead of his boss, and she wouldn't have to remember that she was supposed to be keeping him at a distance.

It wasn't fair of Cal to laugh like that. How could she be expected to think of him as a hired hand, as a temporary employee, when he sat at the end of the table like that, relaxed and at home, pretending to ally himself with the laughing children, his eyes creasing with that devastating smile?

Juliet hoped it would be easier once the children were all in bed, but it wasn't. It was worse. True, there were no twins to make him smile, but there was no Natalie to break the silence with her chatter either. For the first time since she had come to Wilparilla, she wished there was a television, something—anything—to distract her from Cal's still figure.

It had seemed rude not to join him on the verandah after her shower, but now Juliet wished she hadn't. She couldn't think of anything to say. Cal was leaning forward in one of the cane chairs, resting his arms on his knees and turning a beer bottle absently between his hands.

Juliet couldn't keep her eyes off those long, brown competent fingers. They had felt so strong around hers as they had sat by the creek. She remembered them on her arms, sliding to the nape of her neck to hold her head still as he kissed her that first night, and now she couldn't stop wondering how it would feel if he kissed her again.

Would he drop her down to earth, as he had dropped her before, or would he let his hands drift over her, smoothing along her thigh, slipping under her top so that the warm fingers could curve over her breast? At the thought, an involuntary shiver snaked its way down Juliet's spine, and she gulped, dry-mouthed, at her glass of wine, while the silence between them crisped and tightened, like a sharply indrawn breath.

Cal was very conscious of the silence, too. He had been very conscious of everything since Juliet had sat down in the next chair but one. He was glad she hadn't chosen to sit right next to him. Her hair was still damp from the shower and he could smell the shampoo she used. She was wearing some kind of soft skirt and top. Cal hadn't noticed the colour, but he had seen the skirt slither over her legs as she sat down, could almost swear that he had heard it whisper against her body as she shivered.

He had been trying not to look at her. He had been concentrating very hard on his beer. Her presence was tantalising, disturbing. Cal didn't know why she unsettled him the way she did. All he knew was that something about the way she sat there made him think about the silky material lying against her bare skin.

And he knew that if he thought about it much more he would do something that he would regret, like pulling her to her feet and into his arms, like letting his hand smooth insistently over the silk, under the silk, pushing it aside, feeling her skin where the silk had rested...

Cal drained his beer and got abruptly to his feet. 'I'm going for a walk,' he said, in a voice so curt that Juliet looked at him, startled. But before she could ask what was wrong, he had gone, and she was left alone to tell herself that she was glad and to try and forget how he had kissed her once and for all.

Maggie arrived at the end of that week. She was a tall, gaunt woman in her sixties with a gruff, no-nonsense manner that daunted Juliet at first. Cal had picked her up in the plane and brought her straight to the house that Juliet had laboured so hard to clean and paint.

'I hope you'll like it,' she said a little nervously as Maggie's gimlet eyes swept around the pristine rooms.

'It looks fine,' said Maggie.

Fine? Was that all she could say after all her hard work? Indignation made Juliet forget the constraint of the last few days and glance at Cal.

'That means she really likes it,' he said in an undertone as Maggie inspected the kitchen.

Clearly effusiveness was not Maggie's style, but Juliet forgave her everything when she saw her with the twins. She had expected that Kit and Andrew would be as intimidated by Maggie's dour exterior as she was, but they adored her from the start.

'I know,' said Cal, interpreting Juliet's expression without difficulty as they watched the little boys with his aunt. He smiled, and without thinking Juliet smiled back at him. 'I don't understand it either. It's just a kind of magic she has with children.'

Then they realised that they were standing there smiling at each other, and stopped at the same time. Cal went over to join his aunt and Juliet made rather an unnecessary fuss about making some tea.

She was torn between relief at being able to leave the twins in such competent hands, gratitude at having someone to share the housework and cooking, and a feeling somewhere between nervousness and anticipation when she realised that she no longer had an excuse not to spend all her time with Cal.

It had been easy to avoid him over the last few days. Juliet had thrown herself into finishing the house before Maggie arrived and Cal had been busy out on the station. When had met, they'd treated each other with stilted

politeness and kept the conversation so strictly impersonal that Juliet was almost ready to believe that they
had never held hands down by the creek, that she had
never sat on the verandah and fantasised about Cal
slowly taking off her clothes, or wondered if he would
ever kiss her again.

Certainly Cal had never given her any reason to suppose that he would, she admitted half wistfully to herself. It was as if he had erected an invisible and impen-
etrable barrier between them, bristling with unspoken
'Keep Out' signs. It had been easy enough to convince
herself that she had no interest in him other than as an
efficient manager.

And now he had smiled at her again and spoilt it all.

Of course, it was ridiculous to feel nervous about
spending her days with him. It was what she had hired
Cal to do, wasn't it? But it wasn't Cal's detachment that
worried Juliet. It was the strange feeling that fluttered
alarmingly beneath her skin whenever she caught sight
of him, the warm, disturbing sense of something uncurl-
ing deep inside her if her eyes happened to stray to his
mouth or his hands or to the creases fanning out from
the edges of his eyes, as they had a nasty habit of doing.

Cal was finding the prospect of spending all his time
with Juliet equally unsettling. He had been horrified at
how much he had wanted her that evening on the verandah, and had walked for hours before he could trust
himself to go back. Cal didn't want to think what he
might have done if Juliet hadn't gone to bed, if she had
still been sitting there in that damned silk.

He'd wanted to think that it was just the outfit, but
when he'd seen Juliet the next morning, dressed simply
in jeans and a shirt, he'd realised with a sinking heart
that it was more than that. He had to take himself well

away, where he couldn't notice the way her lashes tilted
when she smiled at one of the children, or the fragrance
that lingered in the air long after she had gone.

In the evenings, they had eaten their meal in constrained silence, and then he had made an excuse and
disappeared into the office to deal with the paperwork.
Or pretend to deal with it, while he sat and pictured
Juliet, sitting outside in the quiet night, her legs curled
up beneath her in the chair and her hair curling below
her ear.

It would be easier when Maggie came, Cal had told
himself. Maggie might not be the chattiest of people, but
at least she would be there, and there would be someone
else to look at, someone else to talk to, someone to stop
him making a complete fool of himself over Juliet.

Only now Maggie was here, and Cal realised for the
first time that while the evenings might be easier, getting
through each day was going to be a lot, lot harder.

None of his doubts showed in his face that first morning. To Juliet he looked intimidating and unapproachable
as he drove her out to the airstrip. 'If you want to learn
how to run Wilparilla, you'd better see exactly what
you've got,' he said brusquely, to hide the disconcerting
lift of his heart as she walked out to join him by the ute,
trim in jeans and a dark blue shirt that echoed the colour
of her eyes.

He took her up in the little single-engine plane that
had once been Hugo's. Juliet had been up with Hugo on
a couple of short trips to the nearest town, but she had
never felt safe with him the way she felt instantly safe
with Cal's hands at the controls. He showed her a
Wilparilla she had never seen before as they flew over
the vast brown paddocks with their spindly scrub and
towering termite mounds, along the tree lined creeks and

inaccessible gullies, and across to the wild rocky range where the horizon blurred into a purple haze.

Juliet was intensely aware of Cal sitting so close beside her, of his hands on the joystick, of his eyes narrowed against the glare, of his arm reaching past to point down at a scattered group of cattle that blundered out of the way of the swooping plane. It was all impossibly big, impossibly wild, impossibly beautiful, and she exclaimed in awe and delight as the plane soared up into the dazzling light once more.

'You sound as if you love Wilparilla already,' she said impulsively, constraint forgotten in the sheer exhilaration of the moment. 'How is it you know your way around so well?'

There was no suspicion in her voice, but Juliet's innocent question brought Cal up short. 'I told you, I was brought up not far from here,' he said after a moment. 'I've flown over Wilparilla many times.' It was the truth, but not the whole truth.

Frowning, he banked the little plane until Juliet could look straight down at the red Australian earth below through her side window. He was furious with himself for forgetting everything in his enjoyment of Juliet's pleasure at her first real sight of Wilparilla. He was only here because he wanted Wilparilla back from this woman who sat next to him with her skin warm and glowing in the sunlight and her blue eyes shining. He should be remembering that, not wanting her to see the land as he saw it, not hoping that she understood what it meant to him.

He should be remembering that he had lied to her. That he was still lying. That he had to carry on lying until she was gone.

'We'd better go back,' he said almost curtly.

Juliet didn't want to go back. She wanted to fly on and on with him, high in the sky, where all her doubts and worries evaporated into a tingling sense of happiness, but when she glanced at Cal to tell him how she felt, she saw that his face was set in grim lines that dried the words on her lips.

Puzzled, and obscurely hurt by his abrupt withdrawal, Juliet lapsed back into silence. Cal continued to point out creeks and paddocks as they flew over, but the warmth had gone from his voice, and with it all her pleasure from the flight.

Cal was having to remind himself of all the reasons why Juliet had to be persuaded to leave. Yes, she had had a hard time. Yes, she was a loving mother and kind to Natalie. Yes, she had worked harder than he had expected on Maggie's house. Maybe she *wasn't* quite as selfish as he had thought at first…but she still didn't belong at Wilparilla.

Cal seized on the thought as he brought the plane into land on the bumpy airstrip. Juliet would be much better off back in London. It wasn't as if he was trying to swindle her. He had already offered her a price for Wilparilla well above its real value. If she took it, she could give her sons a comfortable and secure life without wearing herself out on this unforgiving land. He would be doing her a favour if he persuaded her to leave.

No, Juliet would never belong here. So what if she looked just right in a plane, or curled up in one of the verandah chairs, or riding slowly along the creek with Kit perched up on the saddle before her? Those were just the perks of living on a cattle station. Cal prepared to show Juliet the harder side of station life. A week of working with the men would be enough to convince her to give up this perverse idea she had of staying at Wilparilla.

A week later, he had to admit that Juliet had showed no signs of giving up. She had helped with branding and dehorning, been introduced to bull-catching by a wild ringer called Bill, learnt how to drive a tractor and reverse it with trailer, and struggled to mend a fence. Cal had let her stagger under the weight of the wire, and catch her fingers on the barbs until her gloves were torn and her hands bleeding, but not once had Juliet complained.

There had been a stormy look in her eyes now and then, and a decidedly mutinous set to her mouth, but she had known that Cal was testing her, and just when he was sure she was ready to admit defeat, she would press her lips together, grit her teeth and carry on. Cal didn't know whether he admired her spirit or was frustrated by her stubbornness. All he knew was that sometimes—too often—she was close enough for him to be distracted by the smell of soap on her skin, or the pulse beating in her throat, and that Wilparilla seemed to be receding further and further out of reach.

That Sunday, Cal took Natalie riding, as usual, but Juliet and the boys stayed at home. 'I want my daughter to myself,' he said, when Natalie wanted them all to go together.

It struck him as Natalie rode beside him with her bright, animated face how much she had changed since they had come back to Wilparilla. In Brisbane she had been very quiet—polite, but so reserved with the house-keepers that he had employed that he had worried that the time she had spent with only him and the stockmen for company had turned her into too much of a tomboy. Juliet was the last person he would have expected

Natalie to admire, but she had attached herself to her from the start.

'She talks to me properly,' Natalie explained. 'And she smiles with her eyes as well as her mouth.'

Cal could picture exactly what she meant.

'And she smells nice.'

Cal knew that too.

'She's fun.' Natalie peeped a glance at him, and then confessed in a burst of confidence, 'She let me try on one of her lipsticks once.'

'Did she?' Cal's brows rose. He would never have thought Natalie would have the slightest interest in lipstick!

Natalie nodded. 'She gives Kit and Andrew lovely cuddles,' she added after a moment.

Cal heard the unconsciously wistful note in Natalie's voice and his heart cracked. He had done his best for his daughter, but she needed her mother. She had lost more than he had when Sara had died. 'Mum cuddled you when you were little,' he said gently.

She brightened slightly. 'And you did,' she reminded him loyally

'Yes, I did too.'

There was a pause. 'Dad?'

'Yes?'

'Do you think you'll ever get married again?'

Cal stilled. 'Why do you ask that?'

Natalie looked straight ahead, between her pony's ears. 'I just wondered—if you did—if you'd marry someone like Juliet.'

He didn't answer immediately. He had the oddest feeling, as if someone had punched him in the stomach, making it difficult to breathe, let alone talk. 'I don't think Juliet wants to marry anybody,' he said carefully at last.

Natalie looked a little disappointed. 'I think she's sad sometimes,' she confided, and Cal looked down into his daughter's brown eyes and wondered how much she understood.

'I know,' he said. He hesitated, sensing that Natalie's loyalties were torn. He wished that he knew how to explain how he felt about Juliet and Wilparilla. But how could he do that when he wasn't sure how he felt himself? 'I will tell Juliet that we used to live here, Natalie,' he said eventually, choosing his words with care. 'But it might hurt her if I just blurted it out without any warning. I'll tell her when the time is right, I promise.'

Natalie was silent, but Cal thought that she looked relieved. 'Do you wish Wilparilla was still ours?' she asked after a little while.

'Yes,' he said honestly. 'I do.' He ducked to avoid a low branch, remembering how desperately homesick Natalie had been in Brisbane. 'Don't you?'

'Ye—es,' said Natalie hesitantly, 'but if we owned Wilparilla again, Juliet and the twins wouldn't live here, would they?'

Cal felt as if he had walked abruptly into a wall. He had told himself that he just had to think about getting Wilparilla back. He knew that that would mean Juliet leaving, but he hadn't allowed himself to think beyond that, to imagine what it would be like without her, without her smile and her scent and the blueness of her eyes.

'No,' he said slowly, 'I don't suppose they would.'

Natalie would be devastated if Juliet took Kit and Andrew back to London, Cal realised, but what was the alternative? He couldn't stay here as Juliet's hired hand, managing the land that had once been his but with no place in its future, dependent on Juliet's approval. Every sense of pride and independence rebelled at the thought.

If Juliet wouldn't go, then he would give up on Wilparilla, Cal decided as they rode slowly back to the homestead. When the three-month trial was up, he would tell Juliet he didn't want to stay. He would buy another property, start again, give Natalie a new life and a secure future before she got too attached to Juliet and the boys. It wasn't fair to let her hope that they could all stay as one happy family. Even if he had been in love with Juliet—and he certainly wasn't—judging from what she had told him about her marriage, she was unlikely to want to repeat the experience, and he wouldn't risk Natalie's happiness with anyone who wasn't prepared to commit herself completely to him and his daughter.

Or anyone as unsuitable as Juliet, Cal added as an afterthought, with the uneasy feeling that that should have been the first reason he would never even consider marriage with a woman who was—for the time being, at least—his employer.

No, he would give Juliet one more chance to accept how hard the life out here was, one more chance to give in gracefully and leave before it was too late for all of them. He would take her on a muster. There would be no showers or disturbing silk outfits to change into out in the bush. She would be hot, dusty and saddle-sore, and surely after two nights of sleeping in a swag on the ground she would be ready to accept the inevitable.

'Can you leave the twins for a couple of nights?' he asked Juliet that night. She was in her usual place on the verandah, wearing a sleeveless red dress, buttoned at the front from the demure collar to the hem of the long skirt.

There was absolutely nothing provocative about the dress, or the way she was sitting, but Cal still found himself wondering how easy it would be to undo those buttons and slide the dress from her shoulders. He made himself lean against the rail, as far away from her as possible without looking ridiculous.

'I'd have to ask Maggie,' said Juliet, trying not to sound too pleased that he had sought her out. It had been impossible not to notice how he had excused himself every evening after the meal when Maggie left to go back to her house, and although she knew that she ought to have been glad that he was making it easy for *her* to avoid him, somehow it hadn't felt like that at all. 'Why, what's happening?'

'We're going to muster the cattle in from the ranges tomorrow,' said Cal. 'It would be useful if you could come along as well.'

Well, what had she expected? That he was going to suggest a romantic night out alone together under the stars? 'I thought I wasn't useful for anything?' Juliet tried to speak lightly, remembering some of Cal's comments after her attempts at fence-mending, but something that sounded perilously close to disappointment gave an edge to her voice.

'Anyone who can sit on a horse for two days would be useful,' said Cal evenly. 'Do you think you could manage that?'

He had only ever seen her riding that sluggish horse he had provided when they took the twins out. Juliet was looking forward to his face when he saw her ride on her own. She lifted her chin in a way that he was already coming to recognise. 'I expect so.'

'Good.' Cal's face gave nothing away as he leant on the rail, his arms folded across his chest. 'I had a word with Maggie before, and she's happy to stay here until we get back.'

'In that case, I'd love to go,' said Juliet.

They left the next morning on the long ride out to the range, leading a couple of pack horses and others to change for the hard riding the next day. Cal moved to saddle up the slow bay for Juliet, but she shook her head. 'No, I'll take that one,' she said, pointing at a frisky chestnut horse that was sidling away from the sight of the saddles on the fence.

'I don't think that's a good idea,' Cal began, but Juliet already had the horse by its bridle, and before his astonished eyes she had saddled it and had swung herself up onto its back. Wheeling the horse around with a masterful jerk of the reins, she touched its sides with her heels and was cantering out of the yard and down the track after the stockmen.

'Why didn't you tell me you could ride?' he demanded when he finally caught her up.

Juliet slowed the horse to a walk and threw him a teasing glance, blue eyes glinting under her hat. His expression when she rode past him had been everything she had hoped for. 'You didn't ask me,' she pointed out.

'You didn't say,' Cal countered, but he was unable to resist the dancing mischief in her eyes, and in spite of himself one corner of his mouth lifted in a reluctant smile. 'Of course, I assumed that you couldn't ride.'

'You assumed a lot of things about me,' said Juliet, chin lifting in unconscious challenge, and Cal's smile faded.

'You're right,' he said slowly. 'I did.'

There was an odd note in his voice, and Juliet looked at him curiously. His grey eyes were very clear and light in the shadow of his hat, and something in their expression held her fast. Dimly she was aware of the horse moving beneath her, but the reins were slack between her fingers and the open space around them had shrunk until there were just the two of them on horseback, so close that Cal's jeans brushed against hers.

Juliet knew that she should turn her head away, but she couldn't move. She just sat there and looked back into Cal's eyes. It was as if time itself had stopped, leaving her suspended in the dazzling outback light and the outback silence, where the only sound was the slow, insistent beating of her heart and the only reality was Cal, with his quiet face and his cool eyes and the mouth that lurked in her dreams.

The sun beat down around them, and the air smelt of dry grass and dry leaves and dry earth. Juliet's horse snorted at a fly and shook his head, and the sudden movement startled her, breaking the spell. Swallowing, she looked determinedly away.

'I could ride by the time I was the twins' age,' she told Cal, as if that look had never happened, as if her whole body wasn't quivering, acutely aware of everything about him as he rode beside her.

Her voice was high and strained, but she had to keep talking or she would turn and look at him again. 'My father trained show-jumpers, and he put me on my first pony before I could walk. When I first went to work in London, I used to go home almost every weekend to ride, but then I met Hugo and...' She trailed off, shrugged. 'Well, you know the rest,' she said.

'You could have ridden here.' Cal's voice sounded very deep and slow compared to hers.

'Except that I was pregnant soon after I arrived,' she reminded him. 'And later I had the twins. I couldn't ride with a baby in each arm.'

'Couldn't Hugo have looked after the babies for you while you went for a ride?' Cal asked angrily, and then cursed himself as he saw the shadow cross Juliet's face.

'He was hardly ever here,' she said. 'And there wasn't anyone else.'

For the first time Cal realised just how lonely Juliet had been. 'I'm sorry,' he said.

'It doesn't matter now,' said Juliet, determinedly bright. 'I'm riding now.' She looked around her. The bush had expanded back to its usual vast silence, the outline of every tree sharply etched against the brilliant blue sky. 'I've dreamed about this,' she sighed.

Sara had been afraid of horses, Cal remembered, and then felt disloyal. He didn't want to remember Sara's dislike of the bush. He would rather remember how pretty she had been, how open and friendly and wonderfully uncomplicated, and how he had loved her. It was all wrong to realise that she, an Australian born and bred, had never looked as right out here as Juliet did.

He watched her sitting on her horse, perfectly in control, utterly relaxed, letting her body sway with the rhythm of the horse, the shadows from the leaves overhead flickering over her face. How had he ever believed that she couldn't belong at Wilparilla?

The muster was as long and hot and dusty as he had predicted, but whenever he looked at Juliet over the next two days, her eyes were shining.

He saw her emerging from clouds of dust that lay in a fine layer over her skin, and when she took off her hat the dark hair stuck damply to her head. If he had hoped to convince himself that Juliet would never adapt to life in the outback, he knew then that he was doomed to disappointment. She rode long and hard, and did exactly as she was told. When he was discussing plans with the men, she kept in the background, but he noticed that over the three days they rode together she talked to all the men individually. She told him later that it was the

first time she had even learnt their names. At night, when
they sat around the fire, she listened quietly to their sto-
ries, and rolled herself up in her swag without a word
about the hardness of the ground.

Cal was ashamed of himself for being glad that none
of the men had known him as the owner of Wilparilla
and so couldn't tell Juliet the truth that he was increasingly reluctant to confess. He would have to tell her
some time, as he had promised Natalie, but the moment
never seemed to be right, and he didn't want to think
how Juliet would react when she knew.

He was intensely grateful for the presence of the other
men. Something had happened when he and Juliet had
looked at each other. He had felt it, shimmering in the
air, drawing him into her dark blue eyes. Cal didn't
know what it was, but the feeling made him uneasy, as
if he were losing control of everything he had believed
about himself and about her.

It wasn't meant to happen that way. He was ready to
accept that Juliet would stay at Wilparilla and that he
would have to go. All he had to do was stick out the
three-month trial period. There was no point in getting
involved, no point in looking into her eyes, no point in
remembering how it had felt to hold her even briefly.

Cal was careful not to sit next to Juliet when they
stopped for the night, but no matter where he tried to
look his gaze kept straying back to where she sat in the
firelight, drinking billy tea out of a battered enamel mug.
And it was always the time Juliet just happened to be
glancing at *him*, and in spite of themselves their eyes
would meet so that both had to look quickly away again.

Even in the turbulent noise and dust of the muster,
Juliet found herself catching glimpses of Cal, and every
time her heart turned over. She did her best not to meet

his eyes, but she was still excruciatingly aware of him, sitting easily on his big horse, lifting his arm to signal to the men chivvying the cattle along, spurring the horse forward to turn a cow that threatened to break away.

In the end, it was a relief to close the stockyard gate on the last stragglers and leave the cattle milling around, lowing as they raised great clouds of dust with their hooves. Juliet hosed down her horse and led it back to the paddock, and as she came out, she came face to face with Cal. They looked at each other, and something leapt in the air between them, something so urgent and intense that Cal actually took a step towards her.

'Juliet,' he said, in a voice quite unlike his own, but before he could go on, there was a call from behind him, and both of them jerked round as if they had been stung.

'Hey, boss, is it OK if we go off now?'

Juliet swallowed her disappointment and waited for Cal to answer, but he had seen the stockman grinning at Juliet.

'He means you,' he said in an expressionless voice.

Startled, Juliet glanced at the stockman, who was waiting expectantly. She should have been honoured. He was half joking—his way of telling her that she had been accepted—but she could have wept at his timing. 'Of course you can,' she called back awkwardly. 'Thanks.'

He lifted a hand in laconic acknowledgement and strolled off, and she was left facing Cal. 'What were you about to say?' she asked with an edge of desperation.

But the casual way the stockman had called her 'boss' had caught Cal on the raw, reminding him of the reality of the situation. He was Juliet's manager and this wasn't his property any more. 'Nothing,' he said, and his face closed as he turned away. 'Nothing at all.'

CHAPTER SEVEN

HE JERKED his head in the direction of the homestead.
'You go on. I haven't quite finished down here.'

Without another word, Juliet turned and walked away.
Cal watched her go, cursing under his breath. He had
come so close to telling her how much he wanted her,
and then what kind of mess would they have been in?

She was the boss. He had to leave it at that.

'Mummy! Mummy!' Kit and Andrew came running
to meet Juliet as she trudged wearily back to the homestead. Her face lit up when she saw them and she
crouched down to hug them close against her. It didn't
matter what Cal had been going to say. Kit and Andrew
were all that mattered, she thought as she kissed their
small blond heads and walked hand in hand with them
the rest of the way to the house. If they were safe and
happy, that was all she cared about.

Natalie was almost as pleased to see her as the twins
were. She threw herself into Juliet's arms and Juliet
picked her up and hugged her, touched at the warmth of
her welcome. 'Is Dad back?' Natalie asked.

'He's down by the paddock,' said Juliet evenly. 'Why
don't you go and find him?'

She watched Natalie run off and then went in with the
twins to find Maggie. They were all in the kitchen having a cup of tea when Cal appeared, with his daughter
dancing eagerly beside him. He was looking tired, and
Juliet thought his smile as he bent his head to listen to

Natalie was strained. He greeted Maggie, but he didn't look at her at all.

'Cal!' Kit and Andrew scrambled off their chairs at the sight of him and hurled themselves across the room to clutch at his legs.

Juliet watched Cal laugh at their exuberant welcome and hoist them up, one under each arm, while they squealed with delight, and a surge of desire hit her like a tidal wave, blotting out everything else but the longing to go over and touch him for herself, to feel his arms close around and his mouth on hers.

The legs of her chair scraped across the floor as she pushed it back and stood abruptly. 'I'm just going to have a shower,' she said, in a high, unconvincing voice and practically ran out of the room.

She closed her eyes as the water streamed over her, washing off the dirt and dust of the muster, cooling the heat of her skin. She knew instinctively that Cal wanted her, and it was too late to deny that she wanted Cal, but that didn't mean she had to give in to it. Cal just happened to be the first man that had come along, and she wasn't going to sleep with him just because he was available.

She had to think of the boys, she had to think of *herself*. What was the point of getting involved with a man who might want her but who, as far as she knew, didn't even like her very much? A man who would move away as soon as he had bought his own property. A man who would leave her, as Hugo had done, to cope on her own.

The thought of Hugo hardened Juliet's resolve. She wasn't going to let herself be physically or emotionally dependent on a man ever again. Cal was her manager, and that was all he would ever be.

*   *   *

At least Cal made things easier by avoiding her as much as possible over the next couple of days. Juliet used the excuse of the twins' birthday that Sunday to stay at the homestead, saying that she wanted to get everything ready. In truth, all she had to do was bake a cake and wrap their presents, but anything was better than spending all day with Cal, pretending they had never looked into each other's eyes and seen the desire there.

Natalie was more excited about the birthday than the twins, who had been too young the year before to really understand what was happening. She spent days making them a present each, and labouring over a special card for them, and Juliet was touched by her pleasure at being allowed to help wrap the presents Juliet had bought on her last trip to Darwin.

'Dad, can we take the boys swimming at the waterhole for their birthday?' Natalie asked Cal without warning as he walked into the kitchen that Saturday evening.

Cal hesitated. 'I don't see why not,' he said after a moment, glancing at Juliet.

She had turned as if casually when Cal came in, and was studying the kettle with forced interest while she waited for it to boil. If she'd thought about it all, she would have assumed that Cal and Natalie must have found the waterhole on one of their rides, but she was too preoccupied with not thinking about Cal to wonder how they knew about it. His mere presence made her spine tingle, and even with her back turned she could picture him with disconcerting clarity, laying his hat on the side, ruffling his daughter's hair, stooping to greet the twins.

'Kit and Andrew would like to go swimming, wouldn't they, Juliet?' said Natalie eagerly.

Juliet turned reluctantly. 'I don't know,' she began,

knowing that the last thing Cal wanted was to take her anywhere.

'It's quite safe, isn't it, Dad?'

He nodded. 'There are no crocs there. It's a good place for children.'

'The twins would love it,' Natalie persevered, sensing that Juliet was unconvinced.

Juliet didn't have the heart to disappoint her. 'I'm sure they would. That sounds a great idea, Natalie, but there's no need for your father to come on his day off.'

'But Dad's the only one who knows the way,' said Natalie in dismay. 'You want to come, don't you, Dad?' she pleaded.

For a brief moment Cal met Juliet's eyes over his daughter's head, and an unspoken message passed between them. They would do this for the children.

'Of course I do,' he told Natalie. 'Try keeping me away!'

Juliet mustered a smile. 'Shall we take a picnic? Is it far?'

'Too far for the twins to ride,' said Cal. 'I'll drive you there.'

Natalie was thrilled with her idea, and her gaiety was so infectious as they set out the next morning that it was impossible for Cal and Juliet to keep up the strained distance they had been so careful to maintain since the muster.

It's Andrew and Kit's birthday, Juliet told herself. I'm allowed to be happy today. She could go back to being careful tomorrow. Meanwhile, the boys were wildly over-excited with all the attention, Natalie was giggling at their antics, and when she slid a glance from under her lashes at Cal he was smiling indulgently at the noise from the back seat. He had obviously decided to let down his guard for the day.

Juliet relaxed back into the front seat of Cal's four-wheel drive and let her guard down too. Just for the day. Just for the children.

Later, when Juliet looked back on that day by the waterhole, it seemed to her suffused with magic from the start. Her mother had sent the twins water-wings and, egged on by Natalie's promises about the waterhole, they couldn't wait to try them out. Forearmed, Juliet had put on a swimming costume beneath her trousers. It was a bright yellow one-piece, and not at all revealing, she tried to reassure herself as she took off her shirt, but with Cal there she felt as self-conscious as if she had been completely naked. Avoiding his eyes, she took the twins by the hand and ran with them down to the water.

Cal, in the middle of blowing up the last water-wing, watched how the costume clung to her slender curves as she bent, smiling, to say something to Andrew, and the plastic deflated slowly in his hands while he forgot to breathe.

'Dad! Come on!' cried Natalie impatiently, and he swallowed hard and reapplied himself to his task.

He didn't have bathers with him, so he simply pulled off his shirt and waded into the waterhole in his shorts. The water was very cold, and with Juliet looking the way she did, he reckoned that was just as well.

They gave the boys their first swimming lesson, holding them underneath their tummies until they learnt how to kick with their legs while Natalie splashed encouragingly around them. Juliet tried to concentrate on Kit, but she kept catching sight of Cal out of the corner of her eye. He seemed to be outlined against the red rocks behind him, and everything about him stood out in unnatural clarity, the breadth of his shoulders, the texture of his skin, the droplets of water catching in the dark hairs on his chest.

Cal was having just as much difficulty keeping his mind on Andrew. He tried not to look at Juliet, but he knew every time she smiled, every time she shook her damp hair away from her face, or leant away from Kit's inexpert splashing.

Sunlight dappled the water through the trees, but the sun was too fierce for them to stay in the water long, and Juliet laid out the picnic in the shade of the overhanging rocks. Cal stretched out on the rug with a beer while she leant back on her hands and the children bobbed up and down, eating on the move.

Afterwards, the children splashed around in the shallows together, while Juliet and Cal watched them from the rug. It was easier than watching each other. Neither of them spoke. The silence between them seemed to stretch, charged with a simmering awareness.

Cal thought about Juliet, about how near she was. If he stretched out his arm, he could touch her knee. His hand could curve down to her calf, or slide up along the smooth length of her thigh...

Juliet thought about Cal, and the lean strength of his body, so tantalisingly close. She thought about what it would be like to lean over and let her fingers drift over the flat stomach, and then she thought she had better stop thinking about anything at all, and went to join the children, diving into the deep water and letting the cold shock her out of her fantasies.

Watching from the rocks, Cal saw her emerge, gasping. She flicked the hair out of her eyes, and even from a distance he could see the drops of water clinging to her lashes, sparkling like diamonds in the sun. He thought it was probably time to give the twins another swimming lesson. He badly needed a distraction.

Seeing him encouraging Kit, Juliet swam over to help Natalie with Andrew, and for a while they gave a pretty good impression of having absolutely nothing on their minds but teaching two little boys to swim. Juliet even pretended that she had forgotten Cal was there until, stepping back to let Andrew paddle towards her out-stretched hands, she brushed against Cal, who had stepped back at the same time.

Their bodies barely glanced against each other, but they both flinched as if from an electric shock. Juliet half expected to hear a crackle of sparks.

'Sorry—'

'I'm sorry—'

They started to apologise at the same time. Juliet's back was sizzling where Cal's had touched her, and all at once she knew that the pretending hadn't worked at all. It was useless trying to deny the attraction between them any longer, and, when she looked at Cal, she saw the knowledge reflected in his eyes as the air between them jangled with tension.

Juliet looked away first. 'I...I think it's time we went back,' she said in an unsteady voice.

On the surface, everything was the same. Natalie and the twins were cajoled out of the water with the promise of birthday cake, and they drove back to the homestead to the sound of hilarity in the back seat. Maggie came up for the birthday tea, and Juliet was glad that she had invited the stockmen too. They were rather shy at first, but with all the other people around she could avoid Cal and the terrible temptation to reach out and touch him again.

It meant, too, that she could busy herself with the tea,

with lighting two lots of three candles on the cake and supervising the blowing out, which was only achieved with a lot of huffing and puffing. But afterwards, when she put Kit and Andrew to bed, it was harder to distract herself. She bathed them, combed their damp hair and read their favourite story, and all the time the thought of Cal simmered in her mind. Her back still tingled where his skin had grazed hers. She had seen in his eyes then that he wanted her; she knew that she wanted him. The only question now was whether they were going to do anything about it.

Kit and Andrew were tucked into the curve of her body, heads drooping with tiredness but determined to get to the end of the story. Resting her cheek against their hair, Juliet breathed in the warm, rosy, clean smell of her sons and felt guilty about thinking about anything but them.

She lingered in their room until they were asleep, ridiculously nervous about facing Cal alone and wondering how to make it clear that the attraction running between them could not go any further. She even rehearsed a little speech, being very adult about acknowledging the physical attraction but insisting—in the most mature way—on the need to be sensible and think about the children.

As it turned out, she needn't have bothered. When Juliet finally summoned the courage to go down to the kitchen, she found that Cal had invited Maggie to stay for supper. She normally spent Sundays alone in her house, but he had found her dourly clearing away the debris from the tea party and insisted that he would cook something for her for a change.

Juliet wasn't sure whether she felt relieved or disappointed to discover that Cal had arranged a chaperon.

From the dry way Maggie looked between the two of
them, Juliet guessed that Cal's aunt knew perfectly well
why he was so anxious for her to stay, but, being
Maggie, she said nothing.

At least *she* wasn't going to have to say anything
either, Juliet comforted herself as she toyed with the
omelette Cal had made her. He couldn't have made it
clearer that he didn't want to take things any further
either.

'Was it that bad?' he asked, looking at the remains of
the omelette on her plate.

'No.' Juliet flushed. 'No, it was great. I'm just…not
hungry.'

Cal pushed his own unfinished meal aside. 'Me neither,' he said.

Maggie looked from one to the other and shook her
head.

As soon as she had gone, Cal disappeared into the
office, muttering something about paperwork, and Juliet
was left to wash up and reflect that it was all for the
best. Sleeping with Cal would have been a terrible mistake. Everything would have got complicated and awkward, and they would have both ended up regretting it.
Much better to stick with the businesslike relationship
they had at the moment. *Much* better, she told herself
again, as if she hadn't really been convincing enough.

She sat on the verandah for a while, but she couldn't
concentrate on the book she had taken, and in the end
there seemed nothing to do but go to bed. Alone. Juliet
sighed and put the book back on the shelf. She would
have a shower. That might make her stop feeling so
twitchy.

It didn't, but at least she felt clean, she thought as she
dried herself and shrugged on a fine cotton robe. Still

tying the belt around her waist, Juliet walked barefoot down the corridor to check on the twins. They were both sound asleep, and she was smiling as she tiptoed out of their room and turned for her own.

It was then that Cal's door opened.

Cal had done his best to concentrate on the accounts, but Juliet's face kept shimmering between his eyes and the figures. He had waited for Juliet to be safely in bed before he gave up and went to his own room, but he'd been too restless to sleep, and in the end he had got up and pulled on a pair of shorts and a shirt once more. He would go for a walk and try to remember all the reasons why making love to Juliet would be a bad idea.

So he opened the door, and there she was.

Juliet stopped dead at the sight of him, the smile dying from her lips. She hadn't expected to see him, not there, not *now*, and she was seized by something like panic. Unprepared, she could only stare at him with eyes that were huge and dark with desire.

Cal stared back. They had done everything they could to avoid this moment, but here it was all the same, the two of them, alone, wanting each other, with nothing to keep them apart. For Cal it was as if everything that had happened since he came back to Wilparilla had led inescapably to this moment. He couldn't fight it any more, and he didn't want to.

Without a word, without taking his eyes from Juliet's, he stepped back into the room and opened the door wide. She could walk past, or she could walk in. It was her choice.

Juliet knew it too. It didn't feel like a choice, though. It felt utterly inevitable. With an odd, detached part of her mind, she wondered why she had resisted for so long when this moment had been waiting for them all along.

All that agonising, all that frustration, all that pretending that she hadn't wanted this to happen…what had been the use of it all?

There was no point in pretending any longer.

Juliet walked across the corridor and into the room. It was very quiet. Trembling, she stood just inside and waited for Cal to move. Neither of them spoke.

For one terrible moment she wondered if she had, in fact, misunderstood, and that he was working out how to ask her to leave, but after what seemed an age he pushed the door slowly shut with the flat of his hand, and then, just as slowly, he turned the key in the lock. The click sounded preternaturally loud in the silence. Juliet tried to swallow but her throat was too dry, and her legs were trembling so much that she had to lean back against the wall for support.

Cal must have switched off the light as he opened the door, she thought irrelevantly, for the room was dark, lit only by the moonlight shafting through the window that was open behind its wire screen. It was enough for her to see Cal standing before her, not touching her, just looking at her, while the silence strummed around them.

Then, very slowly, he reached out and untied the belt of her robe. Juliet's heart was thudding, her pulse booming with anticipation. She quivered down to her nerve-ends as, still without speaking, Cal slid the robe from her shoulders and let it fall with a soft sigh into a puddle on the wooden floor.

Her skin was luminous in the moonlight, her eyes gleaming pools of darkness in her pale face. Cal stared at her. Her legs were slender, her hips softly curved, her breasts full. She was more beautiful than he had even imagined and he wondered if he was dreaming. Was this really Juliet, warm, breathing, real, *here*?

Juliet couldn't breathe. She was taut, trembling, gripped by a desire so intense that she was convinced that she would simply shatter into a million pieces if he touched her. Terrified that he would, terrified that he wouldn't, when Cal finally let his fingers trace a featherlight line of fire along her collarbone, barely grazing her skin, she caught her breath as if at a shock, but she didn't break.

Instead, Cal kept her in suspense, on the brink of a dizzying freefall of sensation, while his hands drifted enticingly downwards, circling her breasts, teasing over her stomach, smoothing over her hips and thighs and then around to her buttocks and back up her spine until Juliet could bear it no longer. She closed her eyes with a tiny whimper, and as if at a signal Cal closed the gap between them, so that he could press his mouth to the curve of her throat and shoulder.

The touch of his lips sent a shudder of pure pleasure through Juliet, and her arms came up to encircle his body and pull him closer against her. Murmuring her name, Cal kissed the arch of her neck, kissed her throat, her jaw, the pulse-point below her ear, tantalising her, making her wait again, but when Juliet gasped he raised his head and looked down into her dark eyes for one long, timeless moment, before the teasing and the waiting was over and his mouth came down on hers at last.

They kissed with a kind of desperation, as if Cal had been torturing himself as much as her, both goaded beyond the point of resistance by weeks of denying what they had wanted all along. His hands were hard, moving possessively over her body, and Juliet's fingers twisted in his hair as he pressed her back against the wall, kissing her mouth, her cheeks, her eyes, her mouth again.

Juliet kissed him back breathlessly, shuddering at

every touch of his lips, at the sensation of strong hands
sliding up her thigh, lifting her against him. Her fingers
fumbled with the buttons of his shirt, but it took so long
to get just one undone that Cal ended up tearing it off.
Tossing it aside, he pulled Juliet against him once more,
and as her breasts were crushed against his bare chest
the feel of her naked flesh touching his jolted through
her so savagely that she cried out.

Impatiently, she reached for the fastening of his
shorts, but Cal was possessed by the same urgency and
was sweeping her up into his arms, carrying her over to
his bed. He laid her down, resisting her attempts to pull
him down with her until he had stripped off his shorts
himself.

It was all going too quickly, Cal thought. He should
slow things down, make it special for her, for both of
them, but how could he do that when Juliet was reaching
for him and he could feel that her need was as intense
as his own? They had no need to talk, and they had
waited too long for this already.

Juliet smiled as she stretched up her arms to him, and
with a muttered exclamation Cal stooped to kiss her and
let her draw him down onto her. The first unimpeded
meeting of their bodies made her shiver. She was flood-
ing, drowning, dissolving in wave after wave of sensation as their hands moved hungrily over each other. Cal
kissed her throat, her shoulder, her breasts, the satiny
warmth of her stomach until she writhed beneath him,
gasping his name in a way that made Cal lose what little
control he had left.

She was ready for him, though, letting out a sigh of
relief to feel him inside her at last, wrapping her legs
around him as the frantic feeling faded and a new rhythm
took over. They moved instinctively together, slowly at

first, then faster and faster, as the feeling grew in power and intensity, sweeping them up into a great, gathering wave of need so overwhelming that they had no choice but to cling to each other and let it bear them onwards, until it broke at last, and sent them tumbling, spinning, swirling around in a wild, turbulent explosion of release.

Juliet surfaced to a feeling of physical contentment. Her body was sated, her mind wonderfully blank. She didn't want to think; she just wanted to lie there and enjoy the silence. Except that it wasn't silent at all. The air reverberated with the sound of ragged breathing, and it was only slowly that Juliet realised that it was her own. And Cal's.

Insidiously, reality crept back, in spite of her attempts to close her mind to it. More and more details filtered through. She and Cal were lying apart, not touching. There was a faint sheen of sweat on his skin in the moonlight. Oh, God, what had they done?

As if struck by the same thought, Cal swore suddenly under his breath and swung his legs over the edge of the bed so that he could sit up abruptly. Juliet could see the curve of his spine, the hunch of his shoulders as he leant his elbows on his knees and ran his fingers through his hair in a gesture of despair.

Juliet moistened her lips. 'I suppose that was stupid,' she said carefully.

Cal looked at the wall. It hadn't felt stupid. It had felt absolutely right. 'I suppose it was,' he agreed in an expressionless voice.

She wanted to kneel up and put her arms around him, to kiss the back of his neck and urge him down beside her again, to close her eyes and find herself back where she didn't have to think and the only thing that mattered was Cal, his mouth and his hands and the hardness of his body.

But of course she couldn't do that.

Instead, Juliet got up slowly, and went over to pick up her robe, which still lay in a heap on the floor by the door. Cal watched her tie it round her with hands that were not quite steady.

'I'm sorry,' he said.

'You've got nothing to be sorry for,' said Juliet quietly. 'You opened the door and I came in.' She looked down at her hands, wanting to be honest, but anxious to make sure that he didn't think she was going to make a big deal out of it. 'I should thank you.' She tried to smile. 'It's been a long time, as you probably gathered.'

What did she think he was, some kind of gigolo? 'Glad to have been of service,' said Cal, with an edge of bitterness.

'I didn't mean that.' Juliet went over to sit beside him, although not close enough to touch. 'Look, we both know we wanted what happened. I just...don't think we should let it happen again.'

Cal turned to look at her, his body still burning with the feel of her. 'Do you regret it?' he made himself ask.

'No,' she said honestly, 'but I don't want things to change because of it.'

'Nothing's going to change,' he said in a hard voice. 'I'm still your manager; you're still my boss. Or are you afraid I might forget my place?'

Juliet linked her hands together in her lap to stop them shaking. 'No, I'm not afraid of that,' she said with difficulty. 'But I need you as a manager, Cal. That's more important to me than...than...well, you know.'

'Than sleeping with me?'

'Yes,' she admitted, not looking at him.

'You don't need to worry,' said Cal. 'I understand. It was just a physical thing for both of us, wasn't it?'

'Yes,' said Juliet. Aware that her voice sounded a little doubtful, she said it again, more positively. 'Yes, that's all it was.' That was all it *had* been, she reminded herself.

'Then I don't see why we shouldn't go back to exactly the way we were before,' he was saying. 'We'll pretend it never happened.'

'I think it would be best,' she said heavily.

There was a pause. Cal rubbed his hand across his face. He ought to be glad that Juliet wasn't going to make a fuss or turn emotional on him, but instead all he wanted to do was pull her back down onto the bed and kiss her sensible suggestions away.

'Come on,' he said, getting to his feet and helping her up before he succumbed to the temptation. 'You'd better go.'

Unselfconscious in his nakedness, he took her to the door and unlocked it. The sound of the key turning made Juliet ache with the memory of the moment Cal had locked it, when she had known that he was going to make love to her. And now it was over, and she had to leave, when all she really wanted to do was stay.

'Don't look like that,' said Cal, misinterpreting her wistful look. He hadn't meant to touch her at all, but he couldn't resist smoothing a strand of hair tenderly behind her ear. 'It wasn't so terrible, was it?'

'No,' said Juliet. He knew quite well that it had been wonderful.

Cal opened the door. 'Goodnight, then, boss,' he said with a faint smile.

'Goodnight.' Juliet turned to go, then on an impulse

turned back to plant a swift, light kiss at the corner of his mouth. It would be the last time she kissed him, she told herself. 'Thank you,' she said softly, and then she was gone.

CHAPTER EIGHT

JUST a physical thing. That was all it had been. Juliet lay in bed and thought of Cal's lips moving over her skin, his hands tracing patterns of fire on her body, the way he had murmured her name in the dark. She thought about the searing excitement and the extraordinary, marvellous, awe-inspiring joy they had discovered together. She thought about how right it had felt to wind her arms around his neck and kiss him. Just a physical thing.

Nothing to get in a state about.

She wasn't going to be silly, Juliet decided. Cal was a man, she was a woman, that was all. They had scratched that particular itch, and now they could put it behind them. There was absolutely no reason why they shouldn't carry on exactly as they had before. Cal had agreed that they should pretend it had never happened, and Juliet knew that was the right thing to do.

It might be right, but it wasn't easy, as Juliet discovered the next morning. She was excruciatingly aware of Cal as she moved around the kitchen, shaking cereal into bowls for the twins, pretending to listen to Natalie, pretending that everything was normal. The effort left her feeling edgy and irritable, and it didn't help that Cal was just sitting there, eating his breakfast, not revealing by so much as the flicker of an eye that he had possessed her with such urgency the night before.

When Maggie appeared, he got unhurriedly to his feet and carried his plate over to the sink. 'We're loading the cattle onto the trucks today,' he said to Juliet, as if he had never kissed her, never whispered her name against her breast. 'Are you coming, or do you want to stay here today?'

'Of course I'm coming,' snapped Juliet. She didn't want to go at all, but she wanted him to think that she was bothered by last night's episode even less. If Cal wasn't going to feel awkward, then neither was she.

She was given the job of prodding the cattle up the ramp onto the truck, but as they blundered past her her mind kept drifting out of focus and back to the night before, until a shout from Cal would bring her back with a start to the realisation that a cow had balked and was holding up the whole process. She would jab the unfortunate animal with the electric prod and wish that she could move her mind on as effectively.

She had to force herself not to take the easy option and avoid Cal for the rest of the day, but she knew that her voice sounded tight when she spoke to him, and no matter how she tried she couldn't quite meet his eyes. She was dreading the evening, when Maggie went home after supper. If Cal made a move towards her, Juliet knew that she wouldn't be able to resist, for all her grand talk of being sensible. If he took himself off to the office, would she be relieved or disappointed?

In the event, Cal did neither. 'I've been going through the accounts,' he said as he helped Juliet to clear away. 'I think you should consider planting a crop for next year.'

So Juliet had to sit and listen to him talk about sorghum, when all she wanted him to do was to take her down to his room and lock the door as he had locked it the night before. And when he had talked, and she had pretended to listen and agreed to whatever he'd said, he took his papers away, wished her a cool goodnight and went to bed on his own.

As the days passed, Juliet began to feel peeved. Yes, she was the one who had wanted to forget that anything had happened between them, but Cal might at least have had the decency to pretend that he was finding it difficult. Time and again she had to remind herself that she didn't want to get emotionally involved with him, or any other man. The last thing she needed was to find herself in thrall to a mere physical attraction. Cal was her manager, for God's sake! She was paying him to run Wilparilla for her, not to make love to her.

And yet when Cal did just as she wanted, and got on with running the station, instead of relaxing back into the relationship they had had before, Juliet grew increasingly tense. She made a heroic effort to behave as normal in front of the children, although if Natalie's curious looks were anything to go by she wasn't that successful, but when she and Cal were alone she was irritable and snappy, to disguise the way her body still craved his touch, no matter what she tried to tell it to the contrary. She knew that she was being unreasonable, but she couldn't help it. Whoever had said that a taste of honey was worse than none at all had known what they were talking about.

Cal ignored her at first, but a tell-tale muscle began to beat in his jaw. It was hard enough trying to pretend he had never made love to her without Juliet sniping at him. She had wanted him to forget the way she had made him feel that night, but how could he do that when she was always there, when he knew how silky her skin was, how sweet her mouth? She could stick her chin in the air all she liked, but he knew that beneath that haughty exterior burnt a fire and a passion that dried the breath in his throat whenever he thought about it. How was he expected to forget that?

The tension between them twisted tighter and tighter every day, until it exploded at last when Juliet made the mistake of countermanding Cal's decision about the activities for the next week in front of the stockmen. She only did it because he had been treating her as an irritant all week, his explanations about what they were doing and why growing increasingly perfunctory and, to Juliet's over-sensitive ear at least, patronising.

Contradicting him in front of the stockmen was a cheap shot, but she had just wanted to remind him about the situation. As soon as the words were out of her mouth Juliet regretted them, but she was too proud to admit it. Cal's lips tightened dangerously. Curtly dismissing the men, he took Juliet's arm in a steely grip and practically frogmarched her out of hearing.

'Who's running this station?' he demanded, his voice stinging with contempt.

Juliet rubbed her arm resentfully where he had held her, but she wasn't going to be cowed by her own manager. 'I am,' she said, chin lifting in challenge.

'The hell you are!' Cal exploded. '*I* run Wilparilla! You don't know the first thing about it.'

'I know that I own Wilparilla!' Juliet snapped back. 'A fact that seems to have slipped your memory!'

'How could it do that? I'm never given a chance to forget with you looking over my shoulder the whole time!'

'That was part of our agreement—' she began, but Cal wouldn't let her finish.

'We agreed that I would show you what was involved in running a station,' he told her tightly. 'That's what I've been doing, although it would have been a lot easier if I could have just got on and done the job you're paying me to do. As it is, I've turned this station round—and I mean *I've* done it,' he went on, his voice like a lash. 'You've just got in the way.'

Juliet was white with rage. 'I didn't realise I was supposed to go down on my knees and thank you! As far as I'm concerned, you've just been doing what I've been paying you to do. If you're not happy with that, I suggest we call an end to the trial period like now.'

'Is that what all this has been about?' said Cal furiously. 'Push me around and then threaten to sack me when I object—is that the idea?'

'Don't be ridiculous!' said Juliet, turning away, but he caught her arm and pulled her back to face him.

'This is about the other night, isn't it? You've had your thrill and now you're embarrassed about slumming it with me, and you want to get rid of me so you can employ some other fool who'll fall for those big blue eyes.'

The big blue eyes blazed at him. 'How dare you?'

'I dare because you need me a lot more than I need you,' he told her. 'If it wasn't for me, you'd have lost Wilparilla by now, and you know it.'

'Now listen—' Juliet erupted, but Cal stopped her with a finger jabbed against her chest.

'No, *you* listen! I've put up with a lot from you, Juliet, and now I've had enough. If it wasn't for Natalie and Maggie, I'd tell you where you could stick your trial period, but they're happy and settled, and I'm not going to disrupt them before I have to. That means I'm going to stay here until my three months are up, and then I'm going to start looking for my own place, where I can get on with running a successful property without having to kow-tow to you or anybody else.'

He dropped his arm with an exclamation of disgust. 'You can find someone else to be your fancy man when I've gone!' he said, and stalked off after the stockmen without another word, his back rigid with anger.

The atmosphere at supper that night was thunderous. Both were too angry to even make an attempt to be pleasant in front of Maggie, who, after one glance at their faces, resigned herself to a silent meal and escaped as soon as possible.

Juliet stood on the verandah and fought tears of fury, misery and confusion. She wasn't going to cry over Cal. She *wasn't*. So what if he left? She didn't need him, whatever he said. She could find another manager, someone who would get on with the job and not turn her life upside down and then turn round and accuse her of using *him*. How could Cal even *think* she would treat him like that? Juliet choked back a sob. She wasn't going to cry.

Cal, coming back from a futile attempt to walk off his own bitter rage and frustration, saw her standing there, taut as a drawn bow, her arms hugged around herself for comfort. So what if she was lonely and distressed? he asked himself savagely, fully intending to walk past into the homestead, but she turned her head towards him, and the expression in her eyes dissolved the churning anger as if it had never been and left in its place only the knowledge of how much he still wanted her.

Stopped in his tracks, Cal let out his breath in a long sigh of acceptance. 'Juliet,' he said softly, and walked slowly over to stand before her. 'Juliet, why are we doing this to ourselves?'

He reached out and took the arms that she clutched to her in an unconsciously defensive posture, pulling them gently free until he could hold her hands in his warm clasp, and Juliet felt the terrible tension unwinding, unravelling, as he drew her towards him.

'I want you,' he said, his voice deep and low. 'And you want me, don't you?'

He had pulled her into the hard security of his body, until Juliet's face was almost resting against his throat. She nodded, unable to deny it any longer.

'We're not hurting anyone,' Cal went on. 'Why don't we just make the best of what we've got?'

Juliet could smell his skin and feel him breathing, so tantalisingly near that it was hard to think about anything except how her lips were bare millimetres away from his throat. If she leant a fraction closer, she could kiss the pulse below his ear.

'I just... don't want you to think...' was all she could manage, her breath warm against his skin.

'You don't want me to think it means anything?' Cal suggested, when she trailed off incoherently. 'I don't.' His fingers tightened around hers as he bent to kiss her shoulder where it curved into her neck, letting himself smile as he felt her shudder in response. 'Neither of us wants to get involved,' he murmured reassuringly against her jaw.

'No,' breathed Juliet, tipping back her head before the devastatingly gentle touch of his lips.

'It's just between the two of us,' he whispered as his mouth drifted along to her ear. 'We don't need to explain anything to anybody.'

'No,' she agreed, although she hardly knew what she was saying, and cared even less. Cal's soft kisses were sending shivers of delicious anticipation down her spine, and, as if of their own accord, her arms wound round his neck to pull him closer.

'We don't need to change,' he said, reaching the corner of her mouth. 'During the day I'm your manager, you're my boss, but at night… at night, we're just a man and a woman.'

And then, at last, his lips found hers in a dizzying kiss. Juliet melted into him, letting the last lingering doubts dissolve as his arms locked around her and the familiar churning excitement blotted out all other thought.

'Come on,' said Cal raggedly, breaking the kiss with an effort, and he took Juliet's hand to lead her down the corridor to his room. Half-laughing, half-desperate by then, they fell back against the door as he pulled her inside to kiss her once more, and groped behind her to turn the key in the lock.

Much, much later, Juliet sighed and stretched luxuriously beside Cal on the bed. They had made love with a sweetness and a fire that had taken her breath away, just like before, but this time it didn't feel wrong at all. It felt utterly and completely right.

Juliet was floating, awash with contentment. The relief of not having to deny how much she wanted him any more was indescribable. Why had she wasted so much time feeling scratchy and miserable when accepting the inevitable felt so much better? She heaved another long, happy sigh, and turned her head to find Cal watching her indulgently.

'I'm sorry about this afternoon,' she said.

'What happened this afternoon?' asked Cal lazily, unable to think back to a time when he hadn't been able to lie close beside her, not caring as long as she was there, her mouth curving upwards in a dreamy smile that made something ache deep inside him

'We had that horrible argument,' Juliet reminded him. 'It was all my fault,' she said repentantly. 'I was just scratchy and cross because I couldn't forget about the other night, and you could.'

Cal laughed out loud at that, leaning up on one elbow so that he could smooth her hair tenderly away from her face. 'Is that what you thought?' he said. 'That I'd forgotten?'

'If you hadn't, you gave a pretty good impression of it!' she said, trying to whip up some trace of her former resentment, but without much success. 'Anyone else would have said you'd never even met me before.'

Cal looked down at Juliet. Her skin was pearly in the dim light, her eyes soft and dark. 'I tried to forget,' he said seriously. 'I tried because I thought that was what you wanted, but I couldn't. I couldn't forget what it had been like to hold you. I couldn't forget any of it.'

Juliet lifted her arms to pull him down to her for a long, long kiss. She loved his lean, powerful body. She loved the weight of him on her, the taste of his skin and the feel of the calluses on his hand, the way his muscles flexed responsively as she ran her hands over him.

'Forget?' mumbled Cal between kisses as they rolled over, still closely entwined. He tangled his fingers in Juliet's hair and held her head between his hands so that she had to look down into his face. 'No man could forget what you were like that night, Juliet. Why do you think I've been in such a filthy mood all week?'

'I thought it was just because I was being so unreasonable. It was all so stupid,' she sighed. 'First thing tomorrow morning, I want you to tell the men to ignore what I said and do what you wanted them to do originally.'

There was a tiny pause. 'I already did,' said Cal.

Juliet pulled away slightly. 'You what?'

'I've already told them,' he confessed. 'I was so angry

after I'd spoken to you that I went straight back and told them they were to do what *I* told them to do and no one else. I'll take it all back tomorrow,' he added hastily, and stopped Juliet's protest with a kiss.

Mollified, she kissed him back. 'I'm sorry about that argument, too,' said Cal, holding her close. 'I should never have said those things to you. I was just lashing out because I thought you were looking for an excuse to get rid of me.'

Juliet shook her head in baffled amazement. How could he be so blind? But then, she hadn't been thinking that clearly herself, had she? 'I didn't want you to go, Cal,' she said, able to admit it at last. 'I still don't. It's not just because of this,' she added honestly, running her hand over one shoulder, loving the feel of the powerful muscles beneath his skin. 'I know how much I need you to manage the station for me. I couldn't do it on my own.'

'Just as well,' said Cal, smoothing his hand deliciously down her spine and smiling in the way that made her heart turn somersaults. 'Does that mean I get to stay as your fancy man for now?' he teased.

'Well, as long as you give satisfaction...' His accusation had hurt her so much that afternoon that Juliet could hardly believe they were both laughing about it now, as she snuggled down in the curve of his arm and rested her head on his shoulder. His hand moved in lazy caresses over her skin and they lay for a while, warm and relaxed, listening to the sound of their breathing.

'Cal?' Juliet spread her hand over his chest, felt its steady rise and fall.

'Mmm?'

'About that argument...'

He opened one eye and squinted down at her. 'I thought we'd finished with that?'

'I just wanted to know if you meant it when you said I'd been getting in the way,' said Juliet. She had hated the thought of that almost more than anything else.

'Do you want the truth?' asked Cal, in a mock sombre voice.

She swallowed. 'Yes.' Actually, she wasn't sure that she did, but she could hardly say no.

Cal shifted until she lay beneath him. 'The truth is that you've been very useful,' he told her, smiling at her expression when she realised that he had deliberately made her fear the worst. 'You haven't got in the way at all. What you *have* been doing, though, is driving me to distraction, just like you're doing now.'

Juliet stretched provocatively and ran suggestive fingers down his flanks. 'If I really am useful, can I carry on distracting you?'

'You're the boss,' Cal pointed out in amusement. 'You can do whatever you like.'

Her eyes gleamed with mischief as her hands drifted tantalisingly lower. 'So I can,' she said. 'As long as you don't mind.'

'If you carry on doing that, Juliet, I won't mind anything,' he told her, with something between a laugh and a groan of pleasure, and they gave themselves up to the sheer, sensuous pleasure of exploring each other anew.

Afterwards, Juliet lay and savoured the feel of Cal lying heavily on top of her, his face buried in her throat. 'I should go back to my room,' she said reluctantly.

Cal raised his head at that. 'Do you have to go?'

'If I don't, I'll fall asleep, and I don't want Natalie or the boys to see me creeping out in the morning.'

'No, I guess not.' He levered himself away from her

with an unwilling sigh and helped Juliet retrieve her clothes, which lay where they had been discarded long, sweet hours earlier. Then he unlocked the door and took her in his arms for a lingering kiss. 'I'll see you tomorrow,' he said, releasing her reluctantly at last.

She nodded, leaned into him for one last kiss, and then tiptoed down the corridor to her room.

Juliet woke up smiling the next morning. At first the brightness in the room just seemed to be a reflection of her mood as she lay lazily watching the dust twirling in the stripes of sunshine, but when she summoned the energy to look at the alarm clock by her bed her smile turned to a yelp and she sat up abruptly. Half past nine! How had it got to be so late?

Scrambling into her clothes, she hurried down to the kitchen, where she found Maggie with the children. 'I'm sorry I'm so late,' she puffed, still belting her jeans as she bent to kiss the twins and Natalie.

'Cal said to let you sleep,' said Maggie. She was creaming butter and sugar in a bowl. 'He said you were very tired.'

Faint colour touched Juliet's cheeks at the mere mention of Cal's name. 'Er...yes,' she said, hoping that he hadn't told Maggie just why she had had so little sleep.

'They've gone out to fix the pipe at Five Mile Bore, if you want to join them,' Maggie went on, keeping her inevitable conclusions as to the change of atmosphere to herself. 'Otherwise he said he'd see you later.'

'I'll take them out some coffee and biscuits for smoko,' said Juliet.

Cal straightened when he saw the car heading across the paddock towards the bore. He had hoped that Juliet would come. 'Morning, boss.' He smiled as she got out of the car.

'I'm sorry I'm late,' she said, returning his smile demurely. 'I overslept.'

'If you've brought some coffee, you're forgiven,' said Cal, and turned to tell the men to take a break.

'What's the problem?' she asked as she unscrewed the Thermos, and as Cal explained she marvelled at how easy it was to be with him now that she didn't have to deny how much she wanted him any more. His smile had told her everything that she wanted to know, reassuring her that the night before had been as special for him as it had been for her, but that for now he was simply her manager, just as he had said that he would be.

The next few weeks were golden ones for Juliet. Cal never touched her during the day, even if no one else was around. It gave her a secret thrill sometimes to discuss breeding programmes, or the need to order more fuel before the wet, as if they had nothing but a shared interest in the station in common, and to know all the time that once the bedroom door closed behind them he would undress her with deft fingers and pull her down onto his bed.

They made love with a passion that awed and sometimes almost scared Juliet with its intensity. She grew familiar with his body, and would lie counting the creases at the edges of his eyes or the calluses on his hands. She knew exactly how he smiled when she kissed him, knew just where to let her fingers drift to feel his strong, sleek body ripple in response.

Juliet always went back to her own room before the children woke, but she spent longer and longer with Cal every night, bewitched as much by their growing friendship as by the passion they shared. They would lie to-

gether, talking softly in the darkness and smiling as they
felt the other laugh, so comfortable with each other that
the strict boundary they had drawn between night and
day became increasingly blurred.

Cal lay stretched out on his back one night, his hands
behind his head, and wondered out loud about putting
in a new road. 'We'd need a grader, of course,' he said.
'But we could do with one anyway. We could get rid of
that pile of dirt out on—' He stopped, suddenly aware
of Juliet's expression. 'What?' he asked in surprise.

'Nothing.' She smiled wickedly. 'I just love it when
you talk dirty to me!'

Laughing, he moved swiftly to pin her beneath him.
'You should have told me this before, Juliet,' he teased.

'I thought we weren't going to talk about work at
night,' she said, squirming with pleasure as his body
rubbed enticingly against her.

'Who was it who suggested last night that we might
do something to improve the stockmen's quarters?' he
countered. 'And who wanted to know when we'd be
going mustering again?'

'That was just asking questions.' Juliet pretended to
pout. 'Haven't you got something more interesting to
talk to me about than graders?'

Cal pretended to consider. 'Well, there's always the
possibility of planting sorghum next year. I got the feeling you weren't really paying attention when I tried to
talk to you about it before.' His fingers caressed the soft
skin of her inner thigh. 'This might be the moment for
me to go over it again, mightn't it?'

'Yes! Yes!' Juliet wound her arms around his neck in
mock excitement and whispered suggestively in his ear.
'Tell me all about it.'

'Well...' Cal murmured, nuzzling kisses along her

collarbone as she dissolved beneath the ravishing exploration of his fingers. 'We'd have to plough up one of the paddocks,' he began, but Juliet had already stopped listening, and she no longer had to pretend to be excited.

The one thing they never talked about was the future. That would have meant thinking about what they really wanted, and neither Juliet nor Cal were ready to do that. When Juliet wrote to her family and friends in England, she didn't tell them how happy she was. She said that she had found a good manager, and that things seemed to be working out, but that was all. It was almost as if talking about Cal, even writing about him, would break the spell.

From time to time she had felt Maggie's shrewd eyes on her, but if Cal's aunt had guessed what was going on, she kept her opinions to herself. The stockmen, Juliet suspected, neither knew nor would have cared that she and Cal were sleeping together. It wasn't that she felt ashamed at all. It was just a sense that once their relationship was no longer a secret, she would have to admit how she felt about him, and Juliet wasn't sure that she even knew that herself.

She wasn't ready to ask herself how deeply she was coming to rely on Cal. She didn't want to think about what would happen if and when he found a property of his own. It was easier not to think at all, to enjoy things as they were and pretend that they could go on like that for ever.

Cal wasn't anxious to think about the future either. Natalie was happy, he was happy. Aunt Maggie had never been one to give much away, but he knew that she was content as well. He had come to get Wilparilla back, and he couldn't do that now without hurting Juliet.

Some day he would tell her, he promised himself, but not yet. Not yet.

So they closed their minds to the future and gave themselves up to the present instead. The days were long and hot and often hard, but the nights were sweet, and Juliet was happier than she had ever been before. The children picked up on her happiness, and were happier themselves without being aware of it.

Without quite knowing how it had happened, they had fallen into a routine. Sometimes Cal would give the twins their bath, while Juliet listened to Natalie reading, or they would both bath the boys while Natalie perched on the edge and chattered about their day. The weeks were busy, but they tried to keep Sunday free so that Maggie could have a day off. If they went riding, or swimming, they all went together, like a family, but sometimes they would just have a barbecue lunch and catch up with things at the homestead.

One Sunday, Juliet and Natalie were clearing up the kitchen after lunch. Cal had been detailed to keep an eye on Kit and Andrew in the cool, and Juliet could hear the sounds of a rumbustious game going on somewhere down the corridor to the accompaniment of much squealing and laughter. She smiled at Natalie. 'What do you think they're up to?' she said, raising her eyes. 'You'd think they'd be tired, wouldn't you?'

It was only when they had finished the washing up and were putting things away that Juliet realised that the noise had stopped and all was suspiciously silent. 'Go and see what your father's doing with the boys, will you?' she asked Natalie. 'And whatever they're doing, tell them to stop it! They're much too quiet to be up to any good.'

Natalie skipped off and came back a couple of

minutes later. 'Juliet, come and look,' she said. Tugging at Juliet's hand, she led her down to the twins' room, where she laid her finger on her lips and pointed through the open door. Cal was stretched out on Andrew's bed, the two little boys tumbled over him like puppies, and all three of them were sound asleep.

For one terrible moment Juliet thought that her heart had stopped, before it kicked back into its rhythm with a great jolt of emotion. Tears pricked her eyes and her hand closed tightly around Natalie's as she realised for the first time how much she loved them all. Andrew. Kit. Natalie.

And Cal.

CHAPTER NINE

JULIET'S first thought was to wonder how she could not have known she loved him before. She looked at him lying on the bed, his face relaxed in sleep, her sons sprawled trustfully over him, and knew that she had been fooling herself for the past few magical weeks. Of course she had fallen in love with him. How could she not have done?

'We'll let them sleep,' she said quietly to Natalie, and turned away from the door.

She didn't want to be in love with Cal. She had been in love with Hugo, and her fairy tale love had turned into a nightmare of deception and cruelty. Oh, not physical cruelty. Hugo would never have been crude enough to lift a hand, but he had been cruel all the same, thought Juliet. He had taken her innocent adoration and smashed it to pieces. She had been a loving, carefree girl, and he had almost succeeded in crushing the spirit out of her.

Almost, but not quite. The criticism, the careless contempt and the lies had worn her down, until Juliet had believed that she was as worthless as Hugo had said. Kit and Andrew had given her back some confidence in herself, but Juliet never wanted to hurt like that again. Falling in love made you vulnerable, dependent on someone else for your happiness, and she wasn't sure she could go through with it.

But she didn't have any choice. She had fallen in love with Cal anyway, and no amount of hoping was going to change that.

Cal's different, her heart cried. He wasn't anything like Hugo. Where Hugo had made her feel a failure, Cal made her feel as if she could do anything. He made her feel safe; he made her feel sexy. And he didn't lie to her as Hugo had done.

Juliet clutched at the thought for reassurance. No, Cal had never lied. He had been completely honest with her. 'I want you… and you want me…' he had said. 'Neither of us wants to get involved.' He had never pretended that their relationship was anything but physical. He desired her, Juliet hoped he even liked her, but he didn't love her. He had made that clear at the start, and she had no reason to suppose that he had changed his mind.

If only she could go back to the way they had been before! Juliet wished that she had never sent Natalie to see what Cal and the boys were up to, wished she had never seen him looking so right with her sons, wished the realisation of how much she loved him hadn't hit her with the force of a blow.

She wished she could tell Cal that she loved him, but love hadn't been part of their agreement. It might spoil everything if she did that. He might feel awkward, or crowded. Or he might leave if he felt that she was about to pressurise him into a commitment he so plainly didn't want. Juliet didn't think that she could bear the thought of Wilparilla without Cal.

But he might leave anyway, as he had said that he would, and then she would have to bear it. It would be easier if he didn't know that she loved him…wouldn't it?

When Cal woke up from his impromptu nap, Juliet was nowhere to be seen. He found her eventually down by the creek. 'There you are!' he said, spotting her pink shirt through the trees.

Juliet jumped at the sound of his voice, and steeled herself to appear normal by the time he reached her. 'Hi.' She forced a smile. 'Are the boys OK?'

'Natalie's with them.' Cal looked at her closely. 'Is something wrong?'

'No, of course not,' she said brightly, too brightly. 'I just felt like a walk after lunch.' She carried on walking, against the temptation to throw herself into his arms and tell him how miserable and unsure she felt. 'I used to come down here when I wanted to think,' she went on as Cal fell into step beside her. 'I haven't been here for a while. I obviously haven't been thinking too much lately,' she tried to joke.

Cal was seized by a sudden fear that she was going to tell him that she wanted to end their secret relationship. Was she bored? Was he taking too much for granted? 'Sometimes it's a mistake to think too much,' he said.

'I wasn't thinking about anything serious,' she lied. Just about how empty her life would be when he left. She couldn't allow herself to depend on him or she would end up as she had been when Hugo had died: lost, lonely and afraid.

'I just thought that it was time I made an effort to meet other people,' Juliet made herself go on. 'I don't know any of my neighbours apart from Pete Robbins, and I've only spoken to him a couple of times. I suppose I've been waiting for them to make the first moves, but I think now that it's up to me to go out and introduce myself, and let them know that I'm not just like Hugo.'

She hesitated. 'I heard the men talking about the races next Sunday, and I thought it would be nice if we all went. I don't mind driving if you don't want to go,' she added as Cal looked less than enthusiastic.

'No, I'll take you in the plane if that's what you really want,' said Cal slowly. 'I don't think you'll find the races very exciting, though.' He was trying to dissuade her, he realised, not because he didn't think that she would enjoy herself, but because he didn't want her to want to meet anyone else, he didn't want to share her.

Everyone would know him at the races, and he could hardly stop them talking to Juliet. How long would it take Juliet to discover that he was the one who had made the crass offers to buy her out before her husband was cold in his grave? He should have told her long before, Cal realised bleakly. He *would* have told her, but the time had never been right.

The truth was that he hadn't wanted to spoil things. He hadn't exactly lied to Juliet, but he hadn't told her the whole truth either, and he knew that she would be upset when she found out. There hadn't seemed any reason to tell her. He had hardly thought about buying Wilparilla back over the last few weeks. It hadn't seemed to matter who owned the land when he held Juliet in his arms every night, but Cal knew that he had just been fooling himself. Juliet ought to know who he was and what he was doing here.

He would tell her that night, he decided, but Juliet was in an oddly elusive mood. She wasn't hostile, but she seemed to have put up an invisible barrier between them. It left Cal with a cold feeling in the pit of his stomach. Was she trying to tell him that she didn't want him any more? He half expected her to make some excuse to be alone that night, but instead she came to find him on the verandah as soon as the children were asleep. She put her arms around him and held him tightly.

'Let's go to bed,' she said.

She made love with an edge of desperation, and afterwards she cried. Cal held her close, stroking her hair. 'Juliet, there's something I have to say,' he began, but she lifted her tear-stained face and put a hand over his mouth.

'Don't say it,' she begged. 'There's no need to say anything.'

He had guessed that she loved him, Juliet thought wretchedly. It must be obvious how she felt, and now he was trying to remind her gently not to let herself get involved.

She took her fingers from his mouth and sat up, hugging her knees together, not looking at him. 'There's no need to say *anything*,' she said again, desperate to convince him that nothing had changed so that they could carry on as before. 'I...I know this is just a temporary thing for both of us.'

'But, Juliet—'

'So we don't need to explain anything to anybody,' Juliet hurried on. 'You said that right at the beginning, Cal. You said it was just a physical thing, and that's all it is. Neither of us wants to get involved in the kind of relationship where you have to tell all your secrets, do we?'

'No,' Cal agreed slowly. He had allowed himself to forget Juliet's concern not to let anyone close. He had thought they *were* close, but it didn't sound as if she did. Just a physical thing—was that all it was to her?

'Don't tell me anything,' Juliet said, turning back to lean over him. If they got into a discussion about emotions she would give herself away, and she didn't want that. All she wanted right now was to lose herself in Cal's body and pretend for a while that that was all that mattered. She lowered herself until her mouth was just touching his. 'Don't talk at all,' she whispered.

*   *   *

Maggie wasn't interested in the races, she said, so Cal took Juliet and the three children in the plane. The stockmen had left the night before in the ute, and were clearly intending to spend more time in the pub than watching the horses.

There seemed to be more planes than cars parked around the dusty little race course, Juliet thought as they landed. She wished she hadn't insisted on coming, but, having raised the idea, she hadn't been able to think of a convincing reason to change her mind. She would have to face her neighbours some time. Hugo had managed to alienate everyone before she had had a chance to meet them for herself, but it was time she made contact. She might need them once Cal had moved on.

When Cal had gone. Juliet kept making herself think about what it would be like. She was terribly afraid that that was what he had been going to tell her the other night, but he hadn't said anything more. There was a new constraint between them, and the only time it disappeared was when they made love. They would have to talk some time, Juliet realised drearily. Their three month trial was nearly up. Cal would be looking around for a property of his own, and she would have to pretend that she didn't need him and didn't care.

The racecourse consisted of a dusty field behind a rope. There was a beer tent and a token bookie with a blackboard. Juliet remembered going to Royal Ascot with Hugo. She had worn a silly hat and high-heeled shoes and drunk champagne. It was like remembering a film she had seen, a life that had belonged to someone else, not to her.

The children were all excited at the change of scene, but there was a wariness in Cal's eyes that made Juliet uneasy. She felt self-conscious and out of place, even though she was dressed unexceptionably in jeans and a fine linen shirt. She hadn't wanted anyone to accuse her of being overdressed.

'I'll get some drinks,' said Cal brusquely. He disappeared into the beer tent, and Juliet, feeling abandoned, took the children to look at the horses, which were corralled in another patch of dust.

'Did you see Cal's back?' a laconic voice behind her asked.

'Yeah, I heard he was,' answered another.

Back? thought Juliet, then remembered that Cal had told her that he had grown up in the district. 'Coming back' for him could probably mean going anywhere within a five-hundred-mile radius.

'You know he's working at Wilparilla?' the voice went on, and Juliet heard the other man whistle in surprise.

'At *Wilparilla*? Why would he want to do that? I heard he made a packet of money down in Brisbane. He wouldn't need to work for anybody, let alone—'

He broke off as they were joined by another couple, and they moved off, leaving Juliet to wonder why he had been so amazed to hear that Cal was at Wilparilla.

Cal saw Juliet standing stiffly by the rails as soon as he came out of the beer tent. For someone who had professed such an interest in meeting her neighbours, she looked oddly forlorn. Why had she been so keen to meet other people anyway? he thought crossly as he made his way over to her, balancing five drinks awkwardly between his hands. Wasn't he good enough company for her?

'I'd better introduce you to a few people,' he said to Juliet as she handed out the soft drinks to the children. He knew that he sounded ungracious, but he couldn't help it. He wished they hadn't come. He had wanted to stay at Wilparilla, where he could keep her to himself, and now he was going to have to stand there and watch other men look at her.

They wouldn't see what he saw, though. They would see a slender, uptight girl with a rather haughty expression, just as he had seen at first. Only he knew how warm and vibrant Juliet was underneath. She had blossomed over the last few weeks, but something had happened to make her withdraw into her defensive shell again. Cal wished he knew what it was.

Everyone seemed genuinely pleased to see Cal again, Juliet thought as a group hailed him before they had taken two steps. 'Cal, it's good to see you back! We knew you wouldn't be able to stay away. What's all this about you managing Wilparilla? Joe just told me, but I couldn't believe it.'

'It's true enough.' Cal forced a smile. 'And this is my new boss, Juliet Laing.'

There was a startled silence as all eyes swung round to Juliet. What was the big surprise? she wondered as she smiled weakly back at them. Surely it wasn't unheard of for a woman to hire a manager?

Every group they met reacted in the same way as soon as Cal introduced her, with intense speculation swiftly masked by an awkward bonhomie. Juliet was very conscious of people looking after her as she and Cal moved on, and she could feel herself growing more brittle and English by the minute. It was a relief when the races started and there was something else for everybody to talk about. A man standing on a trailer provided commentary through a megaphone, although Juliet couldn't work out how he could tell one horse from the other, as

they all seemed to be enveloped in a cloud of dust
churned up by their hooves.

It was clear, however, that the races were more about
beer and gossip than about horses. After two races, a
break was announced. Juliet slid a sideways glance at
Cal. He didn't look as if he was enjoying this any more
than she was, but perhaps he would have a better time
if she wasn't hanging around him the whole time.

She must be an embarrassment to him, Juliet realised
with a twist of the heart. She didn't belong here, that
was obvious. She was too brittle, too English, too much
Hugo's widow. They were probably all feeling sorry for
Cal, unable to shake off his pathetically clinging employer.

Juliet winced at the thought. 'Come on, boys, let's go
and get another drink,' she said, taking Kit and Andrew
by the hand. Natalie had found some children her own
age almost as soon as they had arrived, and was playing
behind the beer tent somewhere.

'I'll come with you,' Cal began, but he had been spotted already by an attractive woman in a blue flowered
dress who was bearing down on him with a delighted
smile.

'Cal! It's great to see you again. Are you really manager at Wilparilla?'

Juliet slipped away before Cal had a chance to introduce her. She couldn't bear to go through all that incre-
dulity again. What was so strange about Cal being at
Wilparilla?

Kit and Andrew weren't used to crowds, and they
were getting fractious. Juliet got them a drink each and
they pushed their way out of the stuffy tent and found
a place to sit down in its shade instead. It was quieter
there, and out of the way, and there was no one to raise

their brows and stare at her when they learned that she was Cal's boss.

Why would anyone want to stand in the tent, when it was hot and beery and so noisy that the two men on the other side of the canvas were having to raise their voices to be heard? 'Seen Cal?' one shouted, and Juliet sighed. She had overheard enough conversations about how surprising it was that Cal was manager at Wilparilla. She had accepted that it was a temporary measure, until he found somewhere of his own, so why couldn't everyone else?

In the distance, she could see Cal, still talking to the woman in blue. They were obviously old friends. Juliet wondered if the other woman was married. She looked so right standing next to Cal, much more right than she had done. Juliet dug her nails into her palms and looked away, to distract herself by listening to the conversation continuing behind her instead.

'What do you reckon to him managing Wilparilla?' one was saying. 'He must hate that.'

'You know Cal,' replied the other. 'He'll do whatever it takes to get his own way. I don't reckon it'll be for long anyway. The widow's hanging on longer than he thought, but she'll sell in the end and he can get Wilparilla back.'

'Have you seen her?' said the first. 'She's a nice-looking woman. He should just marry her and save his money. I can't believe it hasn't crossed his mind.'

'Maybe she won't have him.'

His friend snorted his disbelief. 'He'd be a good catch. From what I hear, he made a mint of money down in Brisbane.'

'I don't think that would be enough for Cal,' the other man said thoughtfully. 'I've seen her too, and she's nothing like Sara. I wouldn't have said Mrs Laing was his type.'

The first man said something that Juliet couldn't catch, and his companion laughed. 'You may be right, but if you ask me, all Cal is interested in is getting his station back. Wilparilla means more to him than any woman. Want another beer?'

So that was it. Juliet felt sick and very weary. She looked across at Cal, still deep in discussion with his friend in blue, and wondered how she could have missed something so blindingly obvious. She remembered commenting on how quickly he had found his way round Wilparilla, asking if he was hoping to buy a property of his own. Yes, he had said, but he hadn't said that it was *her* station he wanted.

Cal was having trouble concentrating on the conversation. He kept glancing over his shoulder to where Juliet sat with Kit and Andrew in the shade of the beer tent, wanting to go over to her but sensing that he wouldn't be welcome. Now he looked over again, and met Juliet's blue gaze through the crowd. The expression of pain in her eyes cut him to the quick, and he knew instantly what she had discovered. It was the moment he had been dreading all day, and now it was here.

Without even bothering to make an excuse to his companion, Cal went quickly over to Juliet as if afraid that she would bolt from him. But Juliet sat, defeated, just waiting for him. There was nowhere else to go. She looked up at him as he stood before her, her face white with the shock of betrayal. Andrew staggered to his feet and clutched at Cal's hand.

'Can we see horses now?' he asked hopefully.

Cal didn't even hear him. He was looking down at Juliet. 'I tried to tell you,' he said.

'You didn't try very hard,' she said, not even bothering to hide her bitterness.

'Juliet, it isn't what you think,' Cal began urgently, but Juliet was getting to her feet, shaking off the hand he put out to help her.

'I don't want to talk about this in front of the children,' she said, her voice hard. 'I want to go home. Tell Natalie I'm not feeling well, if you like, but go and get her. I'll take Kit and Andrew.'

Kit, hearing the word 'home' began to protest that he wanted to see the horses with Andrew, but Juliet ignored him. Taking the boys firmly by the hand, she walked off to where the little plane was parked with all the others. She held herself rigid, as if it was the only way she could stop herself falling apart.

Cursing his own stupidity, Cal watched her go. He wanted to run after her, to pull her round and make her listen to him, but she was right. He would have to wait until they got home.

It was a silent flight back to Wilparilla. Cal flew the plane, his face grim. Natalie, who had objected to being removed from her game, was sulking, and the boys were tired. Juliet said nothing. She didn't even allow herself to think. Once she started thinking, she knew that the pain would be too much to bear. She just sat there and told herself that she couldn't cry in front of Kit and Andrew.

Somehow Juliet got through the rest of the day. Moving stiffly, like an old woman, she fed the children, bathed the twins, read them a story and tucked them up in bed. Her throat was tight as she bent to kiss them goodnight. Kit and Andrew loved Cal, too. They had learnt to trust him, to treat him as the father they had never had. How were they going to bear it when he had gone? And how was she going to bear their pain as well as her own?

She could hear Cal and Natalie somewhere. Wearily, Juliet went outside and sat on the verandah steps. She could cry now, she thought dully, but the tears wouldn't come. The misery was a tight, hard stone inside her. It wouldn't let her cry.

Cal had lied to her. It was all Juliet could think about. She had worried that he might not love her, but it had never occurred to her that he would lie to her. She had been so sure that he was open and honest. Too honest, she had thought. How stupidly trusting could you get?

She had loved Hugo, and he had lied to her. She had fallen in love with Cal, and now he had lied to her too. She had let herself love him, let herself be happy. She had *trusted* him, and all Cal had wanted was Wilparilla.

Juliet had never felt so betrayed, so lonely, so bereft of anything to believe in. She'd thought she had learnt her lesson the first time, but like a fool she had come back for more. She should have known that the only person she could trust was herself.

When Cal finally came out, she was still sitting at the top of the steps, her head bent and the heels of her hands pressed against her eyes in despair. He could see the nape of her neck, so soft and vulnerable, and the sight of it made something ache inside him.

It was a hell of a time to realise how much he loved her, Cal thought bitterly. He had been a fool. He should have told her from the outset what he was doing at Wilparilla, but he had allowed himself to get carried away. He hadn't wanted to think about anything while he was with her. He hadn't even known that he was falling in love, although now it was hard to believe how blind he had been.

When exactly had it happened? When had he stopped wanting Wilparilla and started needing Juliet instead? Cal looked down at her with a bleak heart. The last thing he had wanted to do was fall in love with her, but he had, and now it was too late to tell her. She would never believe him now.

He sat down next to Juliet on the step, without touching her. She didn't look up, didn't take the hands from her eyes, but she knew that he was there. 'Is it true?' she asked in a muffled voice at last.

'That I used to own Wilparilla? Yes, it's true.'

Juliet's last faint hope that she might have misheard, or misunderstood, died then. She lowered her hands and turned to look at him with eyes that were dull and dark with misery. 'Why did you lie to me?'

'I didn't lie to you,' said Cal heavily. 'I just didn't tell you the whole truth. Everything I told you about selling up, about Natalie wanting to come back—that was all true. I said she wanted to be in the outback again, but she wanted to be *here*, at Wilparilla. And I wanted it too,' he admitted. 'I'd put years of work into Wilparilla. After I left, I kept in touch with people back here. I heard how Hugo was letting everything run down, and I hated the thought of it.'

He hesitated. 'And then Pete Robbins told me that Hugo had been killed.'

'So you thought you'd exploit his grieving widow and pressurise her into selling before she had a chance to know what she was doing?'

'Those offers came from me, yes,' said Cal evenly. 'I couldn't believe that you would really want to stay once you'd lost your husband. I offered you a fair price, more than the land was really worth, but you wouldn't go.'

'And you wouldn't take no for an answer,' Juliet said in a flat voice.

'No,' he admitted. 'I wasn't ready to give up. I still thought you'd change your mind once you realised how difficult it would be for you to run Wilparilla on your own, so I instructed my lawyer to repeat the offer at regular intervals. I was waiting for your reply when I spoke to Pete again, and he said that you were looking for a manager. It didn't sound as if you were thinking of selling, so I decided being manager here would be better than not being here at all. At least I'd be in a position to stop Wilparilla sliding any further downhill.'

Juliet's face was tight, closed. 'And in a better position to persuade me to sell?' she asked bitterly. 'Is that what the last few weeks have been about? Softening me up? Waiting for the right moment to break the news that I don't have any choice but to sell?'

'You know it hasn't been like that,' said Cal with a sigh.

'Do I?' The blue eyes were bright with anger and unshed tears. 'I don't think I know anything any more.'

He ran his hand despairingly over his face. 'Juliet, it *wasn't* like that! I realised on the muster that you weren't going to sell, and that nothing I could do would persuade you otherwise. I'd done my best to make things difficult for you, just to prove to you that you couldn't cope, but you could. You coped with everything I threw at you.'

'So you just changed your mind?' she asked, not bothering to hide her disbelief.

'Yes! I was going to leave when the trial period was up, but then...well, you know what happened, Juliet. You know what it was like. I didn't want to go,' he finished simply.

'Or did you just have a better idea?'

He frowned. 'What do you mean?'

'You'd done a great seduction job,' Juliet pointed out in the same flat, hard voice. 'There must have seemed a much easier way to get Wilparilla back.'

Cal stared at her. 'What are you talking about?'

'Let's face it, marriage would have solved all your problems. It was a good plan, wasn't it, Cal? Marry me—and I'm sure you didn't think you'd have any problem getting me to fall into your arms—and you'd get your precious station back without even having to pay for it, plus a free wife thrown in to look after Natalie *and* sex whenever it suited you.'

A tide of invigorating anger swept through Cal and he surged to his feet. How dared Juliet even suggest such a thing? 'I wouldn't want Wilparilla at that price,' he said savagely. 'The sex has been good,' he told her, matching her deliberate crudity with his own, 'but not that good! I'd rather start again with a new property than tie myself to a woman like you for life!' He looked down at Juliet contemptuously. 'I don't need you, Juliet—I can look after Natalie myself—but you need me.'

'I don't need you!' Juliet shouted in a desperate attempt to convince herself as well as him. 'I don't need anyone!' She clamped her lips together, struggling for control. 'I'll advertise for a new manager,' she said, when she could. 'If it wasn't for Natalie, I'd tell you to leave tomorrow. But for her sake you can stay until your replacement arrives. Then I want you to go.'

Cal's face was set. 'Natalie doesn't need any favours from you,' he said in a biting voice. 'We'll go tomorrow.'

Without another word, he went down the steps and strode off into the darkness. Juliet watched him out of

sight, and then something inside her shattered, and she
buried her head in her arms and wept.

'We brought the mail for you, Mrs Laing.' The stockmen
handed over a bundle of letters sheepishly. They were
late. None of them had been in a state to drive back after
the races had finished, so they had stayed on drinking
and were now suffering from colossal hangovers.

It had seemed like a good idea to stop at the post
office on their way through to pick up the post as a peace
offering, but now it was clear that they needn't have
bothered. Juliet hadn't even noticed that they weren't
there, and, from her expression, she wouldn't have cared
even if she had known they were missing.

Juliet took the letters automatically. She had cried herself out eventually, but when she had dragged herself to
bed she had been unable to sleep. She had just lain there,
curled up as if to ward off a blow, while Cal's final
words hammered in her brain and the knowledge of his
deception raked at her heart.

Her eyes were swollen, and she felt sick and shaky
with misery and the lack of sleep. Maggie had taken one
look at her face when she arrived, and taken the children
into the kitchen. Dimly, Juliet could hear their voices in
the background. Maggie and Natalie must have known
the truth, but they hadn't told her. That hurt almost as
much as everything else.

Never had Juliet felt so lonely or so close to despair.
She sat on the verandah and for want of anything else
to do looked dully through the post. There was a letter
from her mother, a couple from friends, but she didn't
have the heart to open them. The rest were probably
bills, and she couldn't face opening them either. At the
very bottom of the pile was a letter postmarked 'Syd-

ney'. It was the only one that she couldn't identify and she ripped it open incuriously, her mind on Cal. Where was he? What was he doing? Would he really go, as he'd said? And what would she do then?

Survive, Juliet told herself grittily. She had survived alone before and she would do it again. There was nothing else she could do. She had the twins, and she had Wilparilla. She would make it on her own.

Absorbed in her thoughts, she was halfway through the letter before she realised what she was reading, and her eyes darkened with despair. It was from Hugo's parents, the very last people she wanted to hear from. Why did they have to write to her now, of all times? Juliet forced herself to go back to the beginning and read it again. When she had finished she laid it on her lap and gazed unseeingly out at the outback glare for a long time, before she rose stiffly to her feet, fetched her hat and went to find Cal.

CHAPTER TEN

HE WAS down by the stockyards, fixing one of the race gates with a sort of concentrated fury. He looked up briefly as Juliet approached, then went back to wrenching a stubborn piece of metal into position, furious with himself for the instinctive leap of his heart at the sight of her. She looked as bad as he felt, with puffy eyes and misery etched into every line of her face, but her head was still tilted at the gallant angle he loved, and he wanted nothing so much as to put his arms around her and make everything right for her.

Except that he had left it too late for that.

Juliet watched him, choked with conflicting emotions. She loved him, she hated him, she didn't know *what* she felt for him any more. All she knew was that he had lied to her.

She swallowed, looked across at the expanse of empty yards. 'Have you spoken to Natalie yet?' she asked at last. Her throat was so constricted that her voice came out tight and hard.

'Not yet, no.' Cal carried on savagely yanking at the metal with the pliers. He couldn't have explained to himself why he was bothering, but, like Juliet, he hadn't slept the night before and he wasn't thinking clearly. He had been unable to face Natalie that morning, and he had needed to work off his feelings doing something physical. 'Don't worry, I haven't forgotten. I'll tell her when I've finished this.'

'I...I had a letter this morning,' said Juliet, but her

throat closed up completely and she couldn't go on. She could only stand there, looking away from him, her lips pressed together in a straight line while she struggled against humiliating tears.

Cal heard her voice waver and he looked up at her averted face. 'A letter?' he said in a different voice.

Juliet nodded. 'From Hugo's parents,' she managed. 'They're in Sydney. They want to come up and see Kit and Andrew.'

Cal laid the pliers on the gatepost and took off his hat so that he could wipe his forehead with the back of his arm. 'They're their grandparents,' he reminded her.

'I know,' she said, twisting her hands together. 'But you don't know what they're like. They'll come here and they'll hate it, then they'll make me take the twins back to England.'

'They can't make you do anything you don't want to do,' said Cal carefully.

'They can! They can do whatever they want! Look how they packed Hugo and I out to Australia.' Juliet could hear the edge of rising hysteria in her voice, and clamped her mouth shut. She made herself breathe slowly. 'I'm afraid of them,' she confessed, shamefaced. 'I'm afraid they'll try and control the twins' lives the way they controlled Hugo's.'

Cal didn't answer immediately. He had never heard Juliet admit that she was afraid of anything before. 'Can't you tell them it's not a convenient time for them to come?'

'They'll come anyway,' said Juliet. She took a deep breath. 'Cal, you know I...I asked you to leave yesterday?'

Cal would have said that she had told him rather than

asked him, but there wasn't much point in quibbling. 'Yes?'

'I haven't changed my mind,' she said quickly. 'I still think it would be better if you did go but…but would you stay until Hugo's parents have been?' she finished in a rush. 'If there's no manager here when they come, it'll be obvious that I haven't got things under control, and they'll start pressurising me to leave—'

Juliet stopped as she realised what she had said. Why was she asking Cal to help her? He wanted her to leave more than Hugo's parents ever would. 'Forget it,' she said dully. 'It doesn't matter.'

She made to turn away but Cal put out a hand. 'Juliet, wait,' he said, remembering just in time not to touch her. Didn't she know that he would do whatever he could for her? 'I'll stay as long as you want.'

She swallowed. 'Thank you,' she said huskily.

'Can I give you some advice?'

'Not if it's to tell me to give in and sell anyway,' she said, with a flash of her old spirit.

'No, it's not that,' said Cal evenly. 'I was just going to suggest that you arrange to meet Hugo's parents somewhere else. They don't have to come here at all. You could say that you would take the twins to see them, somewhere like the Barrier Reef. It would be neutral territory for all of you, where they could see their grandchildren and you wouldn't have to feel defensive about the way you're bringing them up.'

'I don't want to see them at all,' she said stubbornly. 'They haven't bothered with Kit and Andrew up to now, so why should they suddenly expect to have a say in their lives?'

'You don't know yet that that's what they want to do,' Cal pointed out, wondering how he could be having such a reasonable argument with her when only last night he had been so angry with her he could hardly speak. 'If you don't see them now, you'll always be wondering when they're going to turn up. They won't disappear. They'll always be Kit and Andrew's grandparents.'

Juliet said nothing, but at least she was listening. 'Why don't you take the boys to see them?' he said. 'You're not the girl they knew before, Juliet. You've changed, and maybe they have as well. If anyone knows how hard it is to persuade you to do something you don't want to do, it's me,' he added with a twisted smile. 'You don't need to worry about Hugo's parents making you do anything.'

He glanced at her averted face. 'Have a break, Juliet,' he said gently. 'I know you think I'm prejudiced, but you need to get away from Wilparilla for a bit. Think about things while you're away. I'll look after things here until you get back, and then, if you still want me to go, I'll go.'

Juliet looked down at Wilparilla from the air. She could see the homestead roof flashing in the sunlight, the glint of water in the creek, the wide brown plain, dotted with dusty, spindly trees, stretching out to the shimmering horizon. She was so glad to be home that she wanted to cry.

Juliet couldn't explain why she felt so strongly about this harsh, unforgiving, beautiful land. She knew only that the thought of losing it gripped like a cold hand around her heart. And that the thought of living here without Cal was unendurable.

She had had plenty of time to think over the last ten days. Cal had been right; she *had* needed to get away.

When she had left she had been too raw with hurt and
anger to think clearly, but while she was away she had
lain at night and listened to the sea breaking against the
reef and the truth had seemed obvious. Her need for Cal
was greater than any sense of bitterness. She wanted to
stay at Wilparilla, and she wanted Cal there too.

The previous night, Juliet had walked alone along the
beach and made her decision. 'If you still want me to
go, I'll go,' he had said. Well, she didn't want him to
go, and she was going to ask him if Wilparilla meant
enough to him to marry her for it.

'I wouldn't want Wilparilla at that price.' Cal had said
that too, but Juliet was hoping she could persuade him
that the price was worth paying. So what if she would
know that the land meant more to him than she did?
They would have other things going for them. Their
physical relationship had been fantastic, whatever Cal
said. They had been friends before she had found out
what he really wanted; surely they could be friends
again. Natalie needed a mother, Kit and Andrew needed
a father. Wouldn't it be worth putting their differences
aside to give their children the chance to grow up as a
family?

It had all seemed so reasonable when Juliet had rehearsed the arguments last night, but now, stealing a
sideways glance at Cal's set profile, her doubts resur-
faced. He had met them off the plane at Mount Isa to
fly them back to Wilparilla, but there was a tension about
him that made her nervous. He had managed a smile for
Kit and Andrew, who had thrown themselves at him in
delight, but he had hardly looked at Juliet, and it was
impossible to know what he was thinking.

Cal was a proud man, she reminded herself. What if

he refused? What if he had meant those angry words he had flung at her that terrible night? What if—?

Juliet stopped herself. There was nothing she could do about it now. All she could do was ask him, and if he said no... Juliet couldn't bear to think what would happen if he said no.

Cal made himself concentrate on flying the plane. Juliet had been away for ten days and it had felt like a lifetime. He had been a fool, he knew that now, and he had hurt her in a way she might never forgive. Cal kept remembering the look in her eyes and the way she had turned away from him. How could he have done that to her?

He had hurt Natalie, too. She didn't understand what had happened, couldn't understand why Juliet had taken the boys and left her behind. Every time Cal looked at her, he suffered for her, and his sense of guilt made it hard to bear. All he had wanted was for his daughter to be happy, and he had ended up making her miserable. It was his fault for letting her get close to Juliet when he had known that it could never last.

Cal had spent a hellish ten days trying to comfort Natalie, but unable even to comfort himself. Every day he'd gone out with the stockmen, working on the land, and he'd wondered how he could ever have thought it meant more to him than Juliet. Wilparilla was worthless without her.

He'd ached for her at night and during the day he'd been restless and irritable. He'd kept looking for her, turning every time he heard the screen door bang and willing it to be Juliet.

He could picture her exactly, walking out onto the verandah, shading her eyes with her hand. He wanted to be able to walk over to her and pull her against him, without pretending or waiting until dark. He wanted everyone to know that she was his. He wanted to know that she would always be there.

He wanted to marry her.

Cal was ready to throw pride to the winds. Juliet wanted him to go but he couldn't, not without her. Surely she would see that? If she wouldn't marry him, he would beg her to let him stay on as manager, just so that he could be near her. He would make her change her mind.

Risking a glance at her, Cal saw that Juliet was looking tired and tense. The break didn't seem to have done her much good. If Hugo's parents had been giving her a hard time, it wasn't fair to put any more pressure on her just yet. He would wait until she had settled back at Wilparilla, and then they would talk. In the meantime, it had taken more self-control than he had known not to sweep her into his arms as she came down the steps of the plane.

Natalie was waiting for them at the airstrip with Maggie. She danced up and down impatiently as Cal brought the little plane to a halt, then broke free of Maggie's restraining hold to run across and throw herself into Juliet's arms. 'I missed you!' she said.

'I missed you too.' Close to tears, Juliet hugged the little girl back. Cal watched enviously as he lifted Andrew and Kit down to the ground. It had come to something when you were jealous of your own daughter, he thought wryly.

Even Maggie seemed pleased to see them back. 'And it's been very quiet without you two,' she added as the twins rushed to greet her. They were thoroughly excited to be home, and as soon as they got to the homestead stampeded from room to room, showing off to Natalie.

The three adults were left standing awkwardly in the kitchen. 'What about some tea?' said Maggie after a moment.

Juliet drew a steadying breath. She had to talk to Cal now, before she lost her nerve. 'I'll have some later, thanks, Maggie,' she said, surprised at how normal her voice sounded. 'I...I'd like a word with Cal first. Would you mind keeping an eye on the boys?'

'Of course not.' Maggie looked as if she was about to say something else, but she changed her mind. 'I'll make some tea when you get back.'

Juliet forced herself to meet Cal's eyes. 'Do you mind?'

'No,' said Cal slowly. 'I don't mind.' He wondered if she was going to tell him that she had found another manager. 'Shall we go down to the creek?' he suggested, when Juliet made no move. From the corridor outside came the sound of pounding feet and excited squeals. 'It'll be quieter down there.'

'Yes,' said Juliet gratefully. Now that she had forced herself to the point, she seemed to have run out of steam, and she didn't know what to say next.

They walked down to the creek in silence while she wondered how to begin. She couldn't just blurt out a proposal of marriage. Stooping, she scooped up a handful of dried leaves and crushed them between her fingers so that she could breathe in their dry, pungent scent. Should she just tell him that she loved him? Or would he feel less threatened if she pretended that, as far as she was concerned, marriage was just a practical solution to their difficulties?

Cal watched her, wishing that he could pull her into his arms and kiss the sadness from her face. He knew that she wouldn't believe him if he told her that he didn't care about Wilparilla if he couldn't have her. Even if he left, and tried to woo her from a distance, she would always think that it was the station that he really wanted.

The silence stretched as they stood a little apart, both afraid to start the discussion in case it ended in bitter disappointment, neither able to think about anything else. In the end, it was Cal who broke it. 'How did you get on with Hugo's parents?' he asked.

'Fine.' Juliet turned to face him, not sorry to be diverted from what she had come to say. 'Actually, it was better than fine,' she told him. 'You were right, they had changed. It was a bit difficult at first, but the twins helped. They had a wonderful time, and Hugo's parents loved them.

'I was glad I went,' she went on slowly. 'I went out one day and Hugo's mother was sitting there, just watching Kit and Andrew on the beach, and there were tears pouring down her face. She told me Hugo had looked just like that when he was a little boy.'

Juliet opened her fingers and let the crushed leaves flutter to the ground. 'It sounds horrible, but that was the first time I'd realised what it must have been like for her to lose her son. We talked about Hugo a lot after that. Anne—his mother—told me what a difficult child he had been. They loved him, but they didn't know how to manage him. Every time he did something wrong they felt that they'd failed him, and they tried to compensate by always bailing him out instead of making him face up to what he had done.' She sighed. 'They did their best.'

'It's a pity you couldn't have talked earlier,' said Cal, wondering if this was what she had wanted to talk to him about.

'I think it helped being on neutral ground.' Juliet glanced at him. 'That was your idea.'

'Did they try and persuade you to go back to England?'

'They want me to take the twins back, yes, but they didn't try and force me. They offered to pay for the boys' education and give them some financial security, which is more than I can do.'

There was a pause. 'What did you say?' asked Cal carefully.

Juliet picked up another handful of leaves. 'I said I'd think about it,' she said, without looking at him. It was true. If it didn't work with Cal, she might have no option but to go back to England. But it might not come to that. All she had to do was ask him to marry her.

She drew a deep breath and opened her mouth, but Cal got in first.

'And if you did that, would you sell Wilparilla?' he asked.

Juliet stared at him for a moment, then turned away. All he cared about was buying Wilparilla back. What was the point of asking him to marry her when he so clearly wasn't prepared to share it? She might as well admit defeat now and take the twins back to England, where at least she wouldn't be tormented by memories of Cal at every turn.

'I suppose so,' she said dully, shredding the leaves between her fingers.

Cal took an urgent step towards her. 'Juliet,' he said, 'let me buy Wilparilla from you!'

She gave up then. Opening her hand, she let the last leaves scatter to the ground, like all her hopes. 'All right.'

'You'll sell it to me?'

His eagerness stung her raw sense of hurt. 'Yes!' she cried, stumbling away from him as if he had struck her. 'Yes, if that's what you want, I'll sell.'

She could hear Cal following her and turned her face away, on the edge of tears. 'Go away!' she muttered.

'I haven't finished,' Cal said quietly.

'I've said that I'll sell! What more do you want?'

'I want you,' he said.

There was a long, long silence. Juliet didn't dare let herself believe what she had heard. 'What?' she whispered.

'Juliet, I'm in love with you,' said Cal. Did she really not know? 'I need you. I don't want Wilparilla if I can't have you too. I only wanted to buy it so that you'd know that wasn't why I was asking you to marry me.'

'You want to marry me?' Juliet sounded dazed, disbelieving, terrified that she would wake up and find that this was just a dream.

'Wilparilla doesn't mean anything without you and the boys.' Cal took her hands in an urgent clasp. 'Don't go back to England, Juliet. You belong here, with me.'

Juliet felt the warm strength of his fingers flowing through her as she looked up at him, her eyes huge and blue and starry with tears. She tried to speak but couldn't, and Cal lost his nerve.

'Don't look like that!' he said desperately. 'I never wanted to hurt you, Juliet. I know I should have told you that I was the one who wanted to buy Wilparilla, but I didn't want to lose you. You have to stay here. You *have* to,' he rushed on when she still didn't speak, knowing that he had been a fool, knowing that he *sounded* like a fool.

Afraid that she would simply walk away if he let her go, Cal tightened his grip on Juliet's hands. 'You don't have to marry me. I'll stay on as manager as long as you'll stay. I'll even go if that's what you want.'

Her chest was so tight with swelling emotion that Juliet was finding it hard to breathe. 'I don't want you as manager,' she managed to say at last.

'You want me to go?' Cal's expression was dismayed.

'No,' said Juliet, shaking her head. 'No, I don't want you to go.' She gave him a wavering smile. 'You know I said I wanted to talk to you, Cal?'

'Yes?' he said uncertainly.

'I was going to ask you to marry me,' she told him, her eyes brimming with tears. 'I knew I couldn't bear to be here without you, but then I thought…I thought you just wanted Wilparilla after all…'

The tears spilled over at that, and Cal let out his breath in a long sigh as her words sank in. *'Juliet,'* he said, drawing her into his arms so that he could hold her tight against him, her face buried in his throat, his cheek resting on her soft hair. 'Juliet, darling, I'm so sorry. I didn't know how else to convince you that I love you. I was afraid that otherwise you'd always be wondering if Wilparilla was the only reason I'd wanted to marry you.'

Juliet clung to him, overwhelmed by the feel of his arms around her once again. She had been so afraid that she would have to face life without ever holding him again, and now here he was, telling her that he loved her, and she was so happy that she didn't know why she couldn't stop crying.

Cal kissed her hair as that was all he could reach. 'It's been hell while you've been away,' he said unevenly, as he too let himself believe that everything would be all right. 'We all missed you. Natalie's been desperate, Maggie spent her whole time telling me what a fool I'd been, and even the men kept asking when you were coming back.' His voice dropped. 'But none of them missed you the way I missed you, Juliet. I wanted you all the time. I wanted you with me; I wanted to be able to touch you, to see you smile again.'

Juliet tipped back her head at that, and gave him a watery smile, and he could kiss her at last: a long, long, hungry kiss.

'Oh, Cal, I love you so much,' she mumbled, emerging for breath at one point. 'I can't believe you love me.' Her arms were wound tightly around his neck and she was pressing kisses over his face. 'I've been so miserable since I realised that I'd fallen in love with you. I wish I'd told you now, but I kept remembering that agreement we made. Love wasn't supposed to come into it, was it?'

'We were just fooling ourselves,' said Cal ruefully. 'We never stood a chance. And, talking of agreements, isn't our trial period about over?'

'So it is,' said Juliet, pulling back slightly so that she could smile up into his face. 'I think it's time to make your position a permanent one, don't you?'

Cal laughed and gathered her close. 'Sounds good to me, boss,' he said, and kissed her ear.

'Boss?' She drew away again to look at him quizzically. 'I thought you were going to buy me out?'

'Not completely,' he said. 'I'll buy half the property. That means we'll be equal partners.' He smiled. 'But you'll always be the boss to me!'

'Oh?' she said pertly. 'Does that mean that you'll do whatever I say from now on?'

'Haven't I always?'

Juliet laughed at his expression of mock virtue. 'You could have fooled me! I think I'd like some proof that you're going to do as you're told—and you can start by kissing me again!'

So Cal did as he was told and kissed her, and went on kissing her until the glare went out of the sun. And as it began its slow slide into evening they turned and made their way back along the creek, to the children waiting for them in the homestead.

They were married six weeks later, under the coolabah trees that Juliet had watched so often from the verandah. Her second wedding was very different from her first, Juliet thought happily as she walked down the verandah steps, hand in hand with Cal.

Then it had been a big society wedding. The men had been in morning suits and top hats, and she had worn a long white dress with a veil and an extravagant bouquet of flowers. This time she was wearing a long, sleeveless buttermilk shift made of linen so fine that the slightest breeze lifted it and whispered its softness over her skin. There were side vents up to the knee, but otherwise the dress was utterly plain. Juliet hadn't wanted to spoil its simplicity with any ornaments, but had allowed herself to be self-indulgent instead about the gold strappy sandals. Cal had shaken his head in baffled amusement when he'd discovered that the shoes had cost more than the dress, but Juliet loved them.

It was just after five, and the fierce heat had gone from day. Pausing at the bottom of the steps to put on the soft straw hat that she had bought at the same time, Juliet decided to carry it in her hand instead. She glanced up at Cal, who was unfussily dressed in a pale short-sleeved shirt and moleskin trousers. He had searched through his drawers for a tie, but Juliet had vetoed that. She wasn't used to seeing him in tie, and she wanted him just as he was.

Catching her look, Cal smiled down at her, and Juliet felt the familiar churn of desire. She wished that they were alone, and could go straight back inside to bed, but Cal had insisted on inviting the whole neighbourhood.

'What if they all think I'm just marrying you for your money?' she had asked, suddenly struck by nerves as they'd dressed for the wedding. She'd been sitting in front of the mirror, dithering over which lipstick to wear.

Cal had come up behind her, sliding his hands over her bare honey-coloured shoulders and bending to kiss the back of her neck. 'I've been wondering that myself since you bought those shoes,' he'd teased, and Juliet had tipped her head back in mock indignation.

'Of course, they might all think you're just marrying *me* for Wilparilla,' she'd reminded him.

'We know that's not true, don't we?' Cal had said, dropping a kiss onto her lips. 'You know as well as I do that I'm marrying you for that grader!'

Juliet had laughed and kissed him back. The grader had been her wedding present to him. Cal had given her a beautiful mare of her own to ride, and she already had plans to breed from her.

And the night before, when they'd gone to bed, he had slipped a diamond eternity ring on her finger.

It glinted now in the sunlight as Juliet and Cal walked down to the coolabah trees, where the guests were all waiting for them. The stockmen were there, looking ill-at-ease in their stiff new shirts. There was Maggie, in an uncompromising flowered shirt-waister, and Kit and Andrew, in shorts and white shirts that had been clean when they'd left the house ten minutes ago but which were already distinctly grubby. And Natalie, undoubt-

edly star of the show, in what could only be described
as a pink satin meringue.

Juliet had let her choose own dress when they had all
gone to Brisbane to buy clothes for the wedding. She
remembered being forced into embarrassing brides-
maids' outfits as a child, and was determined that Natalie
would enjoy the day that she was looking forward to so
much. 'You can wear whatever you want,' Juliet had
said generously, but had rather regretted it when, to her
astonishment, tomboy Natalie had fixed instantly on this
pink, frothy confection.

Suppressing a wince, Juliet had exchanged a look with
Cal, who had merely grinned. 'You were the one who
said she needed to be a little girl,' he reminded her.

So Natalie had got her pretty dress, and now stood
proudly by the celebrant. From a distance all that could
be seen of her was her smile. Juliet's heart clenched with
love for her, and her throat was tight with joy as she and
Cal collected Kit and Andrew and went to join her under
the trees.

They'd wanted to be married as a family, with the
three children standing in front of them before the celebrant. Unfortunately, the happy idea was rather marred
by the boys, who were showing off, pushing and shoving
each other beside Natalie until Juliet separated them with
an apologetic glance at the celebrant, who duly paused.
Natalie was given the hat to hold and Kit was sent to
Cal's side, while she took Andrew's hand firmly in her
own. The celebrant suppressed a smile and continued.

After this minor interruption, the brief service went
without hitch, and they were married at last. Radiant
with joy, Juliet smiled at Cal and, unable to wait any
longer, he kissed her. They were both still holding onto
a twin at that point, but the brief kiss they had intended

wasn't enough, and at the same moment they let go of the sticky little hands so that Cal could gather her into his arms for a proper kiss.

Kit and Andrew seized the opportunity to resume their fighting, but Juliet was oblivious by then. She was unaware of anything except the sheer joy of being in Cal's arms and knowing that a lifetime together lay ahead. Cal, too, had forgotten their audience, until Natalie got restless and tugged at his arm.

'Dad!' she said loudly. 'We're all waiting!'

Everyone laughed at that, and a cheer went up as Cal reluctantly released a blushing Juliet. 'They must think that was a hell of a grader you gave me,' he murmured wickedly to her.

Juliet, Maggie and the children had spent the week clearing out the old woolshed. It was many years since sheep had been run at Wilparilla, but the woolshed remained and it was a perfect place for a party. Children ran in and out, and the sound of music and laughter spilled out into the quiet outback night.

It was well past the twins' bedtime, and they were beginning to flag. Juliet, who had been keeping an unobtrusive eye on them as they raced around with the others, touched Cal's arm. 'I think it's time I took the boys to bed,' she murmured.

Cal glanced over at the group of children chasing each other round one of the trestle tables. 'I'll get Natalie and we'll go together.'

Natalie wasn't at all ready to admit that she was tired, but Cal extricated her eventually, and the five of them began to walk back along the track to the homestead. Once they'd left the excitement behind, Kit and Andrew's footsteps began to drag, until Cal picked up one and Juliet the other, and they carried them, the small blond heads drooping against their shoulders.

Walking between them, and swinging off her father's free hand, Natalie was still chattering about the wedding when she interrupted herself with a huge yawn. Cal's eyes met Juliet's over her head and he smiled. 'Time you were in bed too, young lady.'

'Oh, Dad, I don't want to go to bed!' Natalie reached for Juliet's hand. 'I don't have to go to bed yet, do I, Juliet?' she pleaded. 'I've been looking forward to the wedding for *ages* and as soon as I go to bed it will all be over.'

'It won't be over, Natalie,' said Juliet lovingly. 'That's the wonderful thing,' she explained, smiling at Cal with her heart in her eyes. 'It's just begun.'

Kit and Andrew were already half asleep by the time Juliet laid them in their beds. She tucked them in and smoothed the hair from their foreheads as she bent down to kiss them, her heart too full for words. Next door, Cal had persuaded Natalie into bed, too, and she was struggling to keep her eyes open as Juliet kissed her goodnight. Her arms were tight around Juliet's neck as she hugged her.

'It was a good wedding, wasn't it?' she murmured sleepily, and Juliet's eyes stung with tears as she kissed her again.

'It was the best,' she said.

Cal was waiting for her in the doorway. Taking Juliet by the hand, he drew her out of the room and closed the door with a last goodnight to Natalie.

'I suppose we should go back to the party,' Juliet said half-heartedly, but Cal was already pulling her into their room.

'We can go back later,' he said. 'I've had to wait all

evening to get you to myself so that I can tell you how much I love you.'

The door closed behind them, and Juliet melted into his arms. The party, the guests, what everyone would think—all was forgotten as they kissed. And after a while it was Juliet who reached behind her and turned the key in the lock.

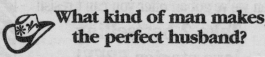

If you enjoyed what you just read,
then we've got an offer you can't resist!

Take 2 bestselling love stories FREE!

Plus get a FREE surprise gift!

Clip this page and mail it to Harlequin Reader Service®

IN U.S.A.	IN CANADA
3010 Walden Ave.	P.O. Box 609
P.O. Box 1867	Fort Erie, Ontario
Buffalo, N.Y. 14240-1867	L2A 5X3

YES! Please send me 2 free Harlequin Romance® novels and my free surprise gift. Then send me 4 brand-new novels every month, which I will receive months before they're available in stores. In the U.S.A., bill me at the bargain price of $2.90 plus 25¢ delivery per book and applicable sales tax, if any*. In Canada, bill me at the bargain price of $3.34 plus 25¢ delivery per book and applicable taxes**. That's the complete price and a savings of over 10% off the cover prices—what a great deal! I understand that accepting the 2 free books and gift places me under no obligation ever to buy any books. I can always return a shipment and cancel at any time. Even if I never buy another book from Harlequin, the 2 free books and gift are mine to keep forever. So why not take us up on our invitation. You'll be glad you did!

116 HEN CNEP
316 HEN CNEQ

Name	(PLEASE PRINT)	
Address	Apt.#	
City	State/Prov.	Zip/Postal Code

* Terms and prices subject to change without notice. Sales tax applicable in N.Y.
** Canadian residents will be charged applicable provincial taxes and GST.
All orders subject to approval. Offer limited to one per household.
® are registered trademarks of Harlequin Enterprises Limited.

HROM99   ©1998 Harlequin Enterprises Limited

HEART OF THE WEST

Every Man Has His Price!

Lost Springs Ranch was
famous for turning young
mavericks into good men.
So word that the ranch was
in financial trouble sent
a herd of loyal bachelors
stampeding back to
Wyoming to put themselves
on the auction block!

HARLEQUIN®
Makes any time special ™

Visit us at www.romance.net

PHHOWGEN

Come escape with Harlequin's new

Series Sampler

Four great full-length Harlequin novels bound together in one fabulous volume and at an unbelievable price.

Be transported back in time with a Harlequin Historical® novel, get caught up in a mystery with Intrigue®, be tempted by a hot, sizzling romance with Harlequin Temptation®, or just enjoy a down-home all-American read with American Romance®.

You won't be able to put this collection down!

On sale February 2000 at your favorite retail outlet.

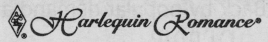
Harlequin Romance®

Harlequin Romance® is proud to announce the birth of some very special new arrivals in:

BABY BOOM

Because two's company and three (or more) is a family!

Our bouncing-babies series is back! Throughout 2000 we'll be delivering more bundles of joy, and introducing their brave moms and dads as they experience the thrills—and spills!—of parenthood!

Our first adorable addition is due in February 2000:

THE BILLIONAIRE DADDY
by Renee Roszel

Look out for other BABY BOOM romances from more of your favorite authors throughout 2000.

Available wherever Harlequin books are sold.

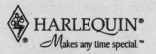